The Hidden Academy

Book 1 of the Shadows of Rebellion series.

by David Lingard

<u>A note from the author</u>

I just wanted to say here, thank you, whoever you are for however you have arrived at this book and my story. It makes a big difference to authors like me, who like to feel as though their hard work and dedication is appreciated when our work is read.

Your investment of your own time and money is as always, well appreciated. It takes a long time and a lot of effort to write, edit and release a book, so please, I ask that you **rate** and **review** everything that you read – and not just this book, so that lesser-known authors can grow their audience and gain the credibility that they deserve.

Also, I have a website that is usually kept up to date with current works, reviews and a few extra little bits. You'll find it at:

Prologue

"You will see tonight, Roderick, my son. A group of mages have promised that they have developed a spell so that we may see your mother again. I know you miss her as much as I do. These mages..."

"Do these mages say that they can bring her back? Do they promise that seeing her will erase the memory of her dying from the sickness that could not be cured?" Roderick asked. His words were not filled with hope but rather scepticism as they often were when his fathers' attention turned to the mages. It was not that Roderick inherently distrusted mages, but he and his father had been promised that mages of Vitalum's Chalice – or life magic - would do everything they could to heal his mother of her sickness. In time, it was clear that these mages would break their promise, and she died without ever seeing the outside of her bedchambers again.

Roderick was still young, not yet even in his twenties, but even in his younger years, he had always wondered if these mages had been overconfident or if this was simply bad luck for everyone involved. It did not matter too much, though; what mattered was that since her passing, Roderick had been lost.

"These mages are practitioners of death magic, and as such they have a far greater understanding of what lies beyond than we will ever hope to grasp," King Cedric replied. "They promise only to allow us to speak to your mother in the beyond so that we may be comforted in her passing." Then the King wrapped an arm around his son, who remained standing to the side. "Besides, the time is now, and once we see your mother again, she will guide us on what it is we are to do next, I am sure of it."

Roderick, though, was anything but sure. He simply couldn't believe that some mages had concluded a spell to speak with the dead; it all just seemed far too convenient to him. The kingdom was at a standstill under his father's mourning, and he had already begun to hear that the citizens were becoming restless, requiring guidance and rule.

"Come now, Roderick, your mother awaits us, and it is best not to keep her waiting; you know how she gets. Then the pair walked into the large circular chamber in the centre of the grand palace.

~

The two mages of the Death Affinity stood facing each other in a dimly lit room before they were to move into the great circular chamber in the centre of the palace, where they would enact their newest spell, though their faces were etched with concern. One, a younger man with short black hair, shifted nervously on his feet while the other, an older man with a long black beard, watched him solemnly. They wore the deep black robes of the Arcani Soul, the death mana, and both of their eyes burned with a deep purple glow. The glowing eyes were the one outward sign that their bodies held mana in one way or another. The Archmage could suppress the glow of the mana that reached his eyes, of course, being able to control its ebb and flow as it circulated his body, but it took effort to do so, and he needed to keep his strength as high as he possibly could before the task to come. The other man, a Master of the Arcani Soul could not yet suppress this ocular glow though his command of the death mana was nothing to be insulted.

"I don't think we should do this, Archmage" the younger Master said, his voice laced with anxiety. "There are too many risks involved, and we don't know what the consequences could be."

The Archmage sighed and rubbed his temples wearily. "I understand your concerns and do not think I do not share in them. But we have no other choice. The King came to us for help, and our order promised to do what we can to bring his Queen back from the dead. This is the best we can do, the solution is not perfect, and the spell can only ever provide a conduit for communication, but we cannot afford to fail. For the good of the kingdom, we must do what we can to help provide a leader who is focussed on doing what is right for his people."

"But what if something goes wrong?" the younger mage persisted. "What if we unleash a power we can't control? The spell has not been tested and we do not know what this amount of power can do."

"Do not worry, young Master," the Archmage replied. "The sanctum has been warded to confine what happens inside, but it is merely a precaution. Nothing will happen with so many skilled mages in attendance." Then he paused for a moment before adding: "And besides, the King is in no state to rule. He needs his Queen to guide him as she has done in the past. Without her, the kingdom lays in a state of perpetual waiting, waiting for decisions that need to be made, decisions in which a King should not delay."

The Master looked down at the floor, his expression troubled. "I just wish there was another way. A new spell that we can't test is so risky."

"I know," the Archmage said, his voice softening. "But sometimes we must make difficult choices for the greater good."

The younger Master nodded, but his eyes remained clouded with doubt. Something was telling him deep down in the pit of his being, where his Arcani Soul swirled, that something terrible was about to happen.

As they both turned to enter the room where the Queen's body lay within her stone crypt, the pair joined the rest of the death mages and completed their circle.

The King and Roderick watched with trepidation as the death mages performed their spell.

The air around them became instantly thick with a heavy, oppressive aura as the mages channel their dark magic. The King, a cautious man by nature, looked on with a mixture of apprehension and fascination plastered across his face, while Prince Roderick seemed tense and somewhat worried, almost eager to see the result.

The air crackled with energy as the mages worked on their spell. The deep purple in all of their eyes shone brightly as though the magic inside of them yearned to escape. The ground began to tremble beneath Roderick's feet, and he took a single small step backwards.

The mages all began to hum as the Archmage stepped forward towards the stone casket with his hands aloft. The hum turned into a chant, and the voices rose to a fevered pitch.

From the Archmage's heart, a purple swirling fog of mana burst forth and floated in the air before his face for a short moment before it began to circle the room, collecting power from within all of the chanting mages as it moved.

Roderick's eyes widened as unease coursed through his body. He sensed something dark and ominous lurking within the spell though he remained silent as he watched. In his father's eyes, he could see hope and anticipation that the spell would be successful and that the Queen would be returned to them once more.

One of the death mages then fell to his knees as the dark mana approached, and his voice broke as he lost focus. Then one by one, the others began to waver as well, their concentration disrupted by the loss of their comrade.

The Archmage stepped forward, his eyes blazing with fierce determination and a brightness that Roderick had never seen before.

"We command you spirit! To give new life to the one you have taken! Give this kingdom new guidance for the future; take pity on this great King and the loss he has incurred!"

The mages had all stopped humming and chanting now, each of them unable to raise themselves from their knees under the weight of the power they were channelling. The King, though, looked as though he was full of glee and excitement.

"Yes! Come back to me, my wife!" Roderick heard his father hiss under his breath, and he moved to take his father's hand, but suddenly, a blinding flash of purple light filled the room, and the ground beneath Roderick shook so violently that it threw him back and away from his father. As he flew, he watched as the purple spectre rushed towards his father and then simply vanished. He felt something touch his very soul and he was abruptly thrown back and to the ground

Roderick watched as his father stumbled backwards, then as though he had been petrified where he stood, the greatest King that the kingdom of Avondale had ever known fell to the ground without ever being released from his sorrow, as he had been promised.

As the light in the room faded and silence returned, Roderick managed to raise himself back to his feet to see the ten death mages lying motionless on the ground, their bodies scorched though not entirely lifeless. His mother's tomb remained untouched as always, but then his eyes fell to where his father lay on the ground.

Roderick rose back to his feet and stepped forward slowly, his eyes wide with wonder and awe. "What have they done?" he whispered, as the King's open eyes refused to focus on anything other than the high domed ceiling above.

Roderick fell to his knees and placed his head on his father's chest, praying to anyone that may be listening for his father to move, to open his eyes, to please, not leave him now.

A mixture of emotions swirled inside Roderick as he sobbed. Horror, shock, and a sense of betrayal all warred for dominance in his mind. But one thing overpowered them all and he raised his head when he realised what it was: The room was filled with the acrid scent of magic, the unmistakable signature of the Death mages who had just struck down his father.

Roderick had always been uneasy around magic, but now his fears had been realised in the most tragic way imaginable. The bright, energetic man who had been his father only moments before now lay motionless on the ground. His life snuffed out by the very force he had been so accepting of, the very force that he had hoped would return love to his heart.

Roderick's mind raced as he tried to make sense of what had happened. He couldn't believe that the mages had turned on his father like this, using their powers to kill him in cold blood. His shock quickly turned to anger, though, as he realised that these magic users had been the cause of his father's death, and the betrayal stung deeply.

The young Prince clenched his fists, his knuckles turning white as he struggled to contain the whirlwind of emotions inside him. He vowed then and there that he would do whatever it took to rid his kingdom of magic to ensure that no one else would suffer the same fate as his father. It was a dark, fateful moment that would shape Roderick's reign as King of Avondale for years to come.

Roderick strode purposefully towards the group of mages as they wearily returned to their feet, his face contorted with anger and wet with tears. "You did this!" he spat at them, his voice ringing out through the chamber and into the halls beyond. "You killed my father!"

The mages stood frozen, their faces pale and fearful as they stared at the young Prince. Then the Archmage stepped forward. "Your Highness, it was an accident, a terrible accident," he began, his voice shaking slightly. "We never meant to…"

But Roderick cut him off with a wave of his hand. "Silence!" he barked. "You will all pay for what you've done. Guards!" he shouted, turning towards the door. "Enter the chamber and kill these mages where they stand. They have killed the King, and they must die!"

The room filled with the sound of clanking armour as the royal guards rushed in, swords drawn. The mages began to panic, scrambling to defend themselves with their magic.

"Please, sire," the Archmage began, but the look that he saw in the young Prince's eyes was one that he knew all too well. Prince Roderick wanted this blood debt paid, and there was nothing that he could say to change his mind. Instead, he stepped to the offensive.

"Your father had forgotten the needs of the kingdom as he mourned the passing of the Queen. He was weak, and his people needed him…"

The Archmage's words were cut short when out of his field of view, Prince Roderick had given the order behind his back to end the life of the treacherous mage. A single bolt from a crossbow within the royal guard whistled through the air and penetrated the mage's heart with a wet thud. The Archmage, the most powerful of the Death mages was no more, felled by a single, tiny construct of man.

The rest of the mages tried to fight back, but it was no use. The royal guard were too well trained and too heavily armed, and they quickly overwhelmed the mages.

Roderick stood back, watching in cold satisfaction as the mages fell one by one, their bodies crumpling to the ground in pools of blood. He felt a sense of triumph and vindication as he surveyed the scene and his heart filled with a newfound determination to rid his kingdom of magic forever.

"Go into the city and kill any mages you find. Destroy their sanctuaries, their shrines and their academies. Magic is now banned in Avondale starting from this very moment as punishment for their crimes against my kingdom," Roderick ordered the Captain of the royal guard. The man simply nodded and left the chamber with his men to spread the word and fulfil his duties.

Five years passed and the kingdom of Avondale had been soundly rid of the mages who had once lived within the walls of the central city. They had found peace within until the day that King Cedric had been killed in a terrible accident, but the new King Roderick had changed all of that. The tyrant King had ordered the deaths of thousands and those who had fled before the full might of his armies could bear down upon them found themselves hunted without reprieve.

Roderick had brought a sense of order back to Avondale where his father had let his duties fall second fiddle to his mourning for his deceased wife, but the cost in lives of such a change had been heavily paid, and the people who called the kingdom their home, lived against a backdrop of fear for what the King could order next, rather than the relative freedoms that King Cedric had allowed. King Cedric had ruled with an open palm and an ambivalent nature, where it was clear from the very beginning of his reign, that King Roderick would rule with an iron fist.

Chapter 1: Discovery

Elara had been only eleven when the kingdom had passed from Cedric to Roderick, and at such a young age, she had never really known what life was like before the change. She had always known that mages and magic was a taboo subject within the city, even as far as the outskirts where she and her two parents lived.

The young girl sat at the worn wooden table, picking at the meagre scraps of food on her plate. She listened to the muffled sounds of the village outside, muffled by the walls of their small farmhouse. It was a sound she knew well, the sound of people trying to survive in a world that was growing increasingly hostile.

Things were not at all as bad as they were in the centre of the city though. The closer you got to the great citadel in the centre, the more often you would hear guards telling people to "open your eyes." It was the way they checked for magic users and the order had become synonymous with the tyrant King's reign.

"Mother, what was it like when the mages were still around?" Elara asked, trying to break the uneasy silence that hung in the air.

Her mother's face tightened as she quickly glanced around the room, checking to see if anyone was listening. Her father grunted and continued to eat his meal in silence, and his eyes focused on his plate as he ignored the question.

"Elara, please don't ask questions like that," her mother replied, her voice hushed. "It's not safe to speak about such things in public, especially with the way things are now."

Elara frowned, pushing her plate away. "But why not? The mages were a part of our history, and I want to know more about them. How can we possibly learn from something if it is entirely erased from history?"

Her mother's eyes flicked towards the door before she leaned in closer to her daughter. "The mages were powerful, too powerful for the likes of the king. He feared what they could do and banished them from the kingdom. Ever since then, things have gotten worse, and the King's grip on the people has grown tighter."

Elara's heart sank as she listened to her mother's words. She had heard stories of the King's tyranny, of how he taxed the people to the brink of starvation and how he punished anyone who dared to speak out against him. But hearing it from her mother made it all the more real.

Her father cleared his throat and pushed back from the table. "Enough of this talk. We need to focus on what we can do to survive, not what we can't change out there in the city. We work as hard as we can, and hope that the soldiers don't take more than we need to survive."

Elara nodded, knowing that her parents were right. They were lucky to have a roof over their heads and food on their plates. But she couldn't help but wonder what it would be like to live in a world where the mages were still around. A world where people had hope and power to shape their own destiny, not the bleak futures that almost all would see laid before them, in poverty and hardship.

Elara remained calm in her contemplation, but she couldn't help but feel a surge of anger at the injustice of it all. "That's not fair! Just because someone is different doesn't mean they should be killed!" she couldn't help but let the anger vocalise itself as the situation churned in her mind. She was about to add more, about how the King was a bully and the like, when her words were cut off as a loud knock echoed through the small farmhouse. Her parents exchanged a worried glance, and her father slowly rose to answer the door. The house became tense as each of the family wondered if they had somehow been overheard and the guards had arrived to accuse them of treason.

Elara listened intently and could hear the muffled voice of a soldier outside, demanding the taxes they owed to the king. She let out a sigh of relief that she was not the reason the guards had arrived.

As her father tried to explain that they didn't have enough to pay what the soldier was asking for, the sum having risen each week for the last few months, the soldier's tone grew harsher.

"Don't try to cheat the King, old man. I can come in and search your home for any valuables you might be hiding. You wouldn't want that, would you?" he asked.

"But I'm telling you, we have almost nothing!" Elara's father protested. "Just look at our house and what we are wearing. We are on our knees…"

"You are on your knees as you should be before the king!" Then he paused and added I'll tell you what? Why don't you just give me everything you can, and we won't say any more about this matter? But next time when a soldier comes knocking on your door, the King expects you to pay what you owe."

Elara felt her blood boil at the soldier's words. How dare he threaten her family! Without thinking, she stood up and glared at him. "You can't just barge into our home and take what you want. This isn't right." Her fists were balled, and her face had turned a bright red as she shouted.

The soldier turned his attention to her, his eyes narrowing. "What's wrong, little girl? Are you hiding something?" the soldier asked. Then he said the three words that sent a shiver through every member of the kingdom. "Open your eyes."

Elara's heart pounded as she realised what he meant. She knew that she had no magic within her, but the words were still terrifying. "I don't have any magic," she said, her voice shaking.

But the soldier wasn't satisfied. "Let me be the judge of that." He took a step towards her, his hand reaching for her face, and again he repeated his order. "Open your eyes."

Elara couldn't help it, she knew she had nothing to hide, but her instincts kicked in, and she shut her eyes as tightly as she could. Then she ran towards the door. It wasn't something that she was used to, but she knew she had no other choice; if the guards even said that they had seen a tiny spark within her eyes, she would be executed, leaving her parents behind to mourn for her.

As soon as Elara felt the cool outside air, she opened her eyes and ran towards the eastern wall that led out past the farmland and into the Forbidden Forest.

She could hear the soldier shouting for the guards along the wall to catch her, but she didn't stop. She ran through her family's farm, her breath coming in short gasps. But it was no use. The soldiers were just so fast, and they soon caught up to her as more guards arrived before her to stop her from leaving.

As the first group of soldiers dragged her back to the farmhouse, Elara knew her life would never be the same. The soldier's words echoed in her head. 'Open your eyes'. The thought made her skin crawl, and she knew she would have no choice but to allow the soldiers to look within her, and she hoped they would find nothing there.

"Please," Elara heard behind her closed eyes. It was the sound of her mother begging. "She is only young, and she is scared. Do not take this out on her. We will pay. We will give you everything we have if you only spare our child."

Elara felt a tight squeeze around her arm. It was not a loving, reassuring action, rather, it was hard and aggressive, and along with it came the three fateful words: "Open your eyes."

Keeping her eyes closed as tightly as she could, the soldier repeated his gruff order, though added: "Or I will open them for you." She knew now that she had no choice.

Her mother had started sobbing as Elara slowly opened her eyes, and the inside of her home came back into focus. She looked at her mother, who was on her knees with her hands clasped together and then to her father, who remained silent in the corner of the room with a soldier standing on either side of him with their swords drawn.

Then her attention turned to the soldier who was peering down at her. He already had one hand on her arm but clasped her other with his other hand tightly as he lowered himself to her head height. She could feel his hot breath as his face came to within an inch of her own, and he peered deep inside her eyes.

Elara stared back at the soldier, searching within his eyes in defiance. His breath smelled like drink, and his eyes were a piercing blue, though as she peered into them, she could see nothing out of the ordinary.

Elara balled her fists and internally willed that her gaze remained dead and focused.

The soldier's eyes flickered as though he had seen something within Elara, and an expression of confusion flashed across his face. Elara's entire body turned ice cold.

Then the soldier stood bolt upright, letting Elara go and turned his attention to her parents.

"No magic within this one," he announced so everyone could hear. "We'll be back in a week, and you can pay double for the trouble you've caused." He announced with a sneer, then walked back through the door, followed by his band of merry asses, their weapons and armour clacking as they walked.

"Elara, you have to be more careful," her mother said as she wrapped her arms around Elara. Her father, though, remained in place in the corner of the room with a terrible expression on his face.

"I do not know how we will afford this tax," he said quietly, looking down at the ground. Neither of her parents had said that this was Elara's fault, though she felt it deep down inside.

The guilt that Elara felt for causing such trouble for her family bubbled in her stomach and pricked the back of her neck. She watched as fear and hopelessness washed over her mother's and father's faces, but she felt something different. She felt determination. Determination to find a way to change all of this, to make a difference in this world, to make things fairer, instead of a constant struggle for those who had little so that they would provide for those with terrible greed.

Elara's guilt, then determination, warred for dominance within her and as she stood and pondered what she could do to help, it turned to burning in her chest. It was as though she had a fire within her, and she immediately began to panic. Wondering if she would fall to the ground, she sat down just in case, but the pain didn't stop.

"Elara? Are you OK?" her mother's words reached her like she was speaking from behind a curtain, and Elara looked up to her mother with a plea for help in her eyes.

"Elara, your eyes!" her mother cried as her eyes met her daughter's. "No! This can't be!

Standing up shakily and walking over to the single mirror within the farmhouse, Elara now saw what had caused her mother to exclaim: staring back at her were her own two eyes, though where they had once been a deep brown hue, they were now ringed with a bright green glow.

"M… mum?" Elara managed to squeak out. "Please… don't let them take me."

Her mother swept across the room in an instant and wrapped Elara up in her arms again. Then her father followed suit, and the three held a tight embrace in the centre of the farmhouse. Her father then spoke for the first time in a long while.

"Whatever it takes, Elara, we will never let anyone hurt you."

Chapter 2: Awakening

Elara sat on the edge of her bed, her mind racing. She had always known that her family was poor, but she had never fully grasped its extent until that soldier came to the door. The heavy taxes they were being forced to pay were crippling, and it was clear that her parents were struggling to make ends meet. She felt so foolish that she had never taken the time to grasp her family's situation truly.

But now there was an even bigger problem. Elara had magic. Earth magic, to be precise as the new green tint in her eyes betrayed. She had always suspected that she was destined for something bigger than being a farmer, wondering what could be as she toiled away at the soil or tended to the animals. Now though, she was certain of it. And she was terrified.

Elara knew that if anyone found out about her new magic, she would be hunted down and killed. The tyrant King had made that very clear. But at the same time, she couldn't just sit back and watch as the taxes slowly destroyed her family. The sensation of feeling powerful but, at the same time, helpless somehow made her feel even worse about the situation. She knew that although some deep power had been awakened within her, for now all it would do would be to make life for both her and her parents very difficult.

Elara's spiralling thoughts were interrupted by a knock on her door. It was her father, and he walked right in.

"Elara, we need to talk," he said grimly.

Elara's heart sank. She knew that they were going to have to talk about her magic at some point, but there was nothing she could say. She hadn't asked for this to happen and everything that her father would have to say would only make things so much more difficult for her.

"We can't stay here," her father continued. "We need to leave before the soldiers come back for the taxes. But we can't take anything with us, or they'll know we've fled. We have to go now while we still have a chance."

Elara felt tears wet her eyes and nodded silently. The sense of panic had begun to rise within her; she hadn't thought that her parents would throw everything away just for her, she thought that her father had come to tell her to run away or that she could go find some uncle that would take care of her. But for all of them to leave their home? It all seemed so much.

But then, where would they go? And what would happen to her magic?

Elara's father told her to pack a single small bag and to join him and her mother as quickly as possible. She packed in silence, though had nothing past a few spare clothes to take with her which she bundled up in a small cloth sack, then she met her parents in the open farmhouse, each of them carrying a small cloth bag of their own.

Her mother met her entrance with a pained smile and the sight of her mother ready to give everything up for her made the familiar pang of guilt burst upwards from her stomach and into her throat.

As they crept out of the house in the dead of night, Elara quickly made a decision. She could not ask her family to do this for her, but she knew that they would refuse if she spoke to them about it. Instead, she would have to leave her family and strike out on her own. She couldn't put them in danger any longer.

At the earliest opportunity, Elara slipped away into the darkness with a heavy heart, not knowing where she was going or what the future held. All she knew was that she had to find a way to survive in a world where magic was a death sentence. Her parents didn't risk calling out for her after they realised she'd disappeared, and she only hoped they would not search for her for too long.

Days passed.

Elara had been on the run for what felt like so long. She had fled eastward, through the huge wooden city gates and into the Forbidden Forest, hoping to find some kind of refuge there. Getting past the guards had been easy; they seldom paid any attention to the citizens on the inside of the wall, and their attention usually turned to keeping any of the creatures of the forest far away from the city.

She had nothing but the clothes on her back, a small amount of food, and the knowledge that she had the power of earth magic within her.

She had entered the forest over a day ago, knowing she had no alternative path.

As she walked deeper into the forest, she couldn't help but feel something within her pulsing as though it knew more about this place than she did. She stopped a few times as she walked when the feeling grew before she realised what this was: her mana within was trying to break free. She tried to figure out what was happening and ask questions inwardly to see if she could divine an answer from whatever the magic truly was, but none came.

On the third day of her journey, Elara stumbled upon a clearing where a group of friendly creatures had gathered. The sight made her smile because as her own food supplies had dwindled to almost nothing, the presence of animals surely meant that food was nearby. The creatures were unlike anything she had ever seen before. One was a tiny, bright blue creature with wings that fluttered like a hummingbird. Another was a fluffy, brown creature that looked like a cross between a rabbit and a squirrel, and as soon as they detected her presence, they were curious about her, peering at her with wide eyes and fascination.

Elara sat down and watched them play, feeling a sense of calm wash over her. She wondered if they knew where she could go to find food or shelter. She tried speaking to them, but they didn't seem to understand her.

Suddenly, a loud roar shook the ground beneath her feet, and before Elara could even think about turning to run, a massive creature burst through the trees, its blazing red eyes immediately fixed on her. It was covered in a mixture of black-grey scales and had razor-sharp claws and the beak of a bird. Elara knew that whatever this creature was, it was not friendly.

The friendly creatures that Elara had been watching quickly scattered, but Elara was frozen with fear. The creature lunged at her before she could even think. She dove to the ground to avoid the strike. The creature rounded on her again, and she knew that simply diving out of the way would not work again.

The creature launched its next attack, and Elara could do nothing but close her eyes and wish for this all to be over before she felt the impact on her body as though a horse and cart had hit her. Then she flew backwards through the air and impacted a very solid feeling tree with an 'oof'. Her vision had already faded from the impact of the creature, but now the impact of the tree on her back had rendered her soundly unconscious, and even if she wanted to turn and run, she knew that she simply could not.

Surprisingly to Elara, a while later, she came to. Her first thought was that perhaps the creature had taken her to its lair to eat later, but that couldn't be true unless the creature had a bed in its lair.

Opening her eyes, Elara could see that she was lying in a bed in a dimly lit wooden room. She could hear the distant sound of hushed voices and the clinking of metal, and sitting up, she rubbed her head, feeling for any signs of cuts or breaks, but after a moment, she could tell that she had made it through the whole ordeal in one piece.

As she now looked around, she realised that she was indeed in a small log cabin, with a fire in the centre and two people standing over what looked – and smelled like a cooking pot.

For the first time in days, Elara felt hope. She knew that perhaps these people were not friendly, but they had saved her from whatever that creature out there was, and she would be forever grateful for that. Plus, she was hungry, and the smell of whatever was in the pot made her mouth water.

Elara sat up in bed, wincing slightly as she rubbed the back of her head and the pain that radiated as she moved. She looked around the small wooden room and saw the two people standing near the cooking pot. As she sat there, they both turned to look at her.

"Who are you?" Elara asked, her voice cracking slightly from disuse.

"I'm Darien, and this is Mara," the man said, gesturing to the woman next to him. "We found you out there in the forest. What are you doing here?"

Darien was a tall, thin man with short-cropped black hair and a prominent nose. He looked to be somewhere around thirty and although he wore a long brown coat, Elara could see that one of his hands were missing. His voice was gravelly, and it looked as though his clothes had been repaired over and over.

Mara on the other hand, was a short and sturdy woman with curly brown hair pulled back into a braid. Her features were small and sharp and the expression she wore on her face said that she was not someone to be messed with. Her clothes were also worn and repaired, and it made Elara wonder how long these people had been out in the Forbidden Forest.

Elara hesitated, unsure if she should trust these strangers. But she knew she had to get to somewhere safe, and maybe they could help her. "My name is Elara. I need your help. I've just had some magic, or mana awaken in me… I think? My eyes are green now and if they find me within the city then I'll be executed."

Darien and Mara exchanged a look. "You want to get to the Academy then?" Mara asked.

"The Academy?" Elara asked, then putting two and two together, she added: "If I have magic, and I need to learn how to control it, then the

Academy is probably where I should be headed." Then added: "I can't stay here. The guards will find me."

Darien nodded in understanding. "We know where the Academy is," Darien said. "But it's not safe to go there. The King's army has been searching for it for years and eventually he will find it."

"I don't have a choice," Elara said. "I need to go there. Please, can you take me?"

Darien hesitated for a moment before nodding. "We'll take you," he said. "But you need to know that the journey won't be easy. And we'll only take you as far as the entrance. You'll have to find your own way inside."

Elara nodded. "Thank you," she said. "Will they teach me how to cast spells there?"

Mara nodded this time. "They'll teach you how to cast spells, but unless they do something a bit more proactive, then there won't be an Academy for much longer!"

"What?" Elara asked, but Darien shook his head at the woman.

"Now isn't the time," he said sternly, and Mara looked away. "Try to eat something, the forest isn't exactly the safest place, and if you don't keep your strength up, it could swallow you whole."

"What was that thing?" Elara asked as she pushed a spoonful of soup into her mouth after Darien had passed her a bowl.

"That was a Grimscale," Darien replied nonchalantly. "Not a very big one, but still dangerous if you don't know what you're doing. Best to keep out of their way."

"But what is it exactly?" Elara asked again.

This time Mara replied. "Creatures that have absorbed far too much ambient mana. They're twisted by it. It wasn't a problem in the past, but as magic was pushed from the kingdom, it's congregated, focussed and that's why you'll find things here that you couldn't have imagined were real."

"Oh come on Mara," Darien objected playfully. "It's not all that bad. Yeah, some things look a bit scary and there's plenty that'll kill you if they had the chance, but mostly the forest's harmless, as long as you know where you're going."

Elara breathed a silent sigh of relief. Mara's words had indeed worried her, but Darien had managed to diffuse the situation.

"Come now, we'll take you once you're finished," Darien added.

Once they had left the wooden cabin and re-entered the Forbidden Forest and began walking, Darien and Mara leading the way, Elara listened intently as they explained to her about their destination

"We noticed that your eyes are green, but they're not as bright as ours.

That's because we're Journeyman rank mages, and you're just an Apprentice – well almost I guess," Darien said. "As your command over your mana – what you will soon learn is called 'Gaia's Grace', increases, you will advance in rank and your eyes will become brighter and more vibrant."

Elara nodded, taking it all in. She felt a sense of excitement and purpose she hadn't felt in a long time. With Darien and Mara's help, she was already one step closer to mastering her magic and finding her place in the world.

"Can you do magic?" Elara replied in wonder as she took in the beauty of the forest all around her.

"We can," Darien answered, but Mara interrupted him.

"But we only do it if we really need to," she said. It sounded strange to Elara, but she wouldn't argue the point.

As they walked on, Elara could feel the mana pulsing through the forest and it seemed to be thickening somehow, and a part of her wondered if she could ever learn to wield it properly like she suspected Darien and Mara could.

"Careful where you step," warned Darien. "The ground here is treacherous, and it's easy to get caught in a trap set by the fae."

"The fae?" asked Elara, intrigued.

"Yes, they're mischievous creatures who love to play tricks on humans," explained Mara. "If you're not careful, they could lead you into a trap or a dead end, and you could be lost forever in this forest."

Elara shuddered at the thought and looked around, trying to spot any signs of danger. She saw a tree that looked like it was about to move, but then she shook the thought from her head, berating herself.

"That's a Living Tree," Darien said, gesturing to the tree. They're ancient guardians of the forest, and they can be fierce if they perceive a threat to the forest, but if you're respectful and ask for their help, they can be great allies.'

Elara nodded silently, not wanting to admit that she had first thought the tree looked like it would move but that she'd also internally dismissed that as preposterous.

As the group continued walking, Elara saw a beautiful creature with a human-like body and deer antlers. "What's that?" she asked, pointing at it.

"That's a dryad, a nature spirit.," said Mara. "They can be friendly or hostile, depending on their mood, so it's best to be cautious around them.'

Then as they approached a clearing, Elara's ears picked something up that she hadn't noticed before. It was a beautiful melody, sung in a tone that was almost imperceptible, though now that she'd heard it, it was getting louder and louder, drawing her towards it.

"That's the song of the nymphs," said Darien before Elara even had the chance to ask. "They're ethereal creatures that embody the beauty and harmony of nature. If you're on your own and let your mind wander, they can lure you in and you'll be done before you know it."

"You don't want to be eaten by one of those," Mara added with a scoff. "But just talking to another person generally wards off that racket."

"There's a lot to remember here," Elara said cautiously. "How do you do it?"

"Don't worry, you get used to it," said Darien.

"And if you don't," Mara added, "you won't be around long enough to have to worry!"

Darien shook his head to himself. "Listen, just try not to make too much noise or touch anything you don't know what it is. The big ones to watch out for are the werewolves and the griffins, but they're big and loud, other than that, you'll be fine."

Elara clicked her tongue and her eyes widened somewhat. She hadn't even thought about the werewolves yet.

As they walked deeper into the forest, Elara began to notice that the trees around them had started to become larger, older even, as though this part of the forest had stood for much longer than the rest. The trunks were wider, their bark rough and gnarled, and the branches extended high into the sky like outstretched fingers. And then, after what felt like hours of walking, they arrived at a clearing.

In the centre of the clearing stood a large stone structure, with a wooden door carved into the side. The door was adorned with intricate patterns and symbols, and at its centre was a tree, etched into the wood as if it were growing there. Elara couldn't help but stare, her heart pounding with excitement.

Darien and Mara exchanged a knowing look, and then turned to Elara. "This is it," Darien said, gesturing to the door. "The Academy of earth magic."

Elara stepped forward, her hand hovering over the door. She felt a strange sense of reverence, as if she were about to enter some sacred place. And then, with a deep breath, she pushed the door open.

Beyond the door, a long stone staircase ran down and away from her, deep into the ground until it met the flickering light of a burning torch.

Elara turned to Darien and Mara before she took a single step inside, thanked them sincerely for their help, then took her first step into her new life.

"Uh, you didn't see us," Darien said as he turned away and again Elara nodded.

Once she had walked down the staircase, Elara could hear the faint murmur of voices coming from down the hall, and her heart swelled with excitement at the thought of finally being among other mages like herself.

"Hello?" She called out ahead of her and the voices abruptly hushed.

"Hello?" She repeated loudly, and then she heard the footsteps coming towards her.

As the footsteps grew louder, Elara felt a wave of nerves wash over her. She didn't know what to expect from the mages in this place and suddenly the idea of meeting other mages was daunting. But as the figure rounded the corner, she could see the relief on his face at the sight of her.

"Welcome to my Academy," the man said, a warm smile on his face. "I'm Arin, and I am the Archmage, and Headmaster here in the Academy."

Elara returned the smile, feeling a sense of belonging wash over her. "Thank you," she said, her voice filled with gratitude. "My name is Elara and I've been searching for this place… I lost my home and…" she couldn't help but feel her eyes welling with tears as she spoke, but Master Arin held up a hand to stop her.

"Yes, we tend to keep a low profile. But we're always happy to welcome new mages."

Chapter 3: The Hidden Academy

Elara's gaze couldn't help but drift towards his vibrant green eyes, which seemed to glow with an inner light. She knew that such bright green eyes must have been the tell-tale sign that Master Arin was a very powerful mage, and she wondered what kind of spells he was capable of.

"Welcome to our humble Academy, Elara," Master Arin said, his voice deep and resonant. "As I said, I am the Headmaster around here, and it is my pleasure to show you around and explain everything about our Academy."

Elara nodded, feeling a rush of gratitude towards Master Arin for giving her this opportunity. She wasn't sure what an Archmage was, but it seemed like he was the top man in the Academy. Whatever it meant, she was sure that if she wanted to learn magic, then this was certainly the person to teach her.

"Shall we begin?" Master Arin asked, gesturing for Elara to follow him.

Elara's heart surged at the Master's words.

"Now? I'm… I'm going to learn magic now?" she asked, her eyes widening.

Master Arin chuckled, then said: "No, not quite yet. First, let me show you to your room. I believe it is almost ready. But don't think that this is what I usually do around here, you just happened to be very lucky to catch me as you entered."

As soon as Elara began to follow the Master down the tunnel that seemed to be lined with thick, twisted roots to hold the soil back, she could feel something inside her resonating with the place. It was as though it had a heartbeat, and that it was perfectly in tune with her own. She felt alive like never before.

As the pair walked, Master Arin began to explain more about the Academy. "This Academy was grown magically, deep underground, in a hurry, you must understand. It is not perfect as I am sure you will discover,' he said. "It was a desperate measure to protect and teach all of the mages with Gaia's blessing like yourself during a time of great danger. We lost far too many of our number over the last few years and I can only hope that what we have done here has helped as many as was possible."

Elara listened intently, her curiosity growing with every word. She had never heard of anything like this before, and she couldn't help but think about Darien and Mara who clearly had some issues with this place.

"Each room is grown from the roots that come down into the Academy, shaped by earth magic we wield," Master Arin continued. "It makes for a unique and comfortable living environment, and we take great pride in our use of natural resources. We've actually gotten pretty good at it if you ask me," he added, looking around appraisingly.

Passing rows upon rows of polished wooden doors, each with a beautiful, shining tree etched upon them, Master Arin eventually stopped before a door that had the number one hundred and forty-two carved into it.

"I think this one will do," Master Arin said with a smile. "Just place your hand flat against the door and we'll see what we can do."

Elara didn't know exactly what was happening but followed the instruction without hesitation.

The door felt cool and very solid to her touch, and she looked questioningly at Master Arin.

"Now, you need to nurture the mana within you. Gaia's Grace is a gift that has many uses and you must learn to control it. Do you feel the mana within you?" Master Arin asked.

Elara nodded.

"Good, now I want you to imagine that the mana within you is a tiny seedling placed deep within your heart."

Elara did as she was told and visualised her mana as a tiny green seed, sat in the centre of her heart. It was an odd sensation, as the visualisation paired with the feeling of the actual mana inside her seemed to somehow just make sense.

"Now…" Master Arin instructed. "Imagine your seedling growing roots. Roots that will encompass your heart, entwining with your physical body."

As the Master spoke, Elara followed the instructions again as best she could. She pushed at the edges of the seed within her and visualised it growing as she had been told. Then suddenly she realised that the tiny seedling within her was moving. It was subtle, almost unnoticeable but it was definitely happening.

Her arms tensed against the wooden door and sweat began to bead on Elara's forehead.

"The seed grows just as your control will grow. Do not stop, put all of your effort into growing this seedling. Nurture it, care for it and one day it will grow into a mighty oak," Master Arin said. "Now push a little harder, put all of your effort into growing that seed."

Sweat ran down Elara's face as she redoubled her effort. She closed her eyes tightly and as her arms began to shake and her body felt heavy, suddenly she felt a pulse of magic burst free from her chest. The feeling was nothing short of magical.

Elara's eyes snapped open, worried that she had somehow managed to accidentally hurt the Master, though he simply looked down at her with a warm smile.

"And that is how you claim this room for your own," Master Arin said, gesturing to the door that was now open a few inches. "It is your own space and none other than you will be allowed to enter, that is without your say so of course. Please, feel free to make yourself comfortable, and when you are ready, feel free to explore the Academy."

Elara smiled weakly at the Master, unable to speak. She watched him walk away and then turned her attention to the open door, pushing it open and stepping inside.

The room was simple, yet beautiful. The walls and floor were made of earth, and the roots that snaked through the room were adorned with bright white flowers. There was a comfortable looking bed in the corner, a desk and chair, and even a small fireplace.

"This is incredible," she whispered to herself, unable to contain her awe.

Elara spent some time exploring her new room, taking in every detail of the simple yet beautiful space. She sat down at the desk and ran her fingers over the smooth wooden surface, imagining all the things she could learn and discover in this Academy. The memory of how her mana had felt within her though, didn't leave her for a second.

After a few minutes, she stood up and made her way towards the door, sure that she had learned everything that the room had to offer, and eager to explore the rest of the Academy. As she stepped into the hallway, she saw that Master Arin had been right – the Academy was huge. The hallway stretched out before her, lined with doors just like hers, each one with a tree etched onto it, but all of them shut.

Elara took a deep breath and began to walk down the hallway, marvelling at the intricate designs on the walls and ceiling that were either formed from, or etched into the roots that constituted the place.

As she walked, she eventually heard the sound of laughter and conversation coming from one of the rooms. This door though, unlike the others was open a crack and curious, she pushed open the door and peered inside.

The room was filled with people, all chatting and laughing together. They were mostly younger boys and girls, around Elara's age and they turned to look at her as she entered. She felt her cheeks flush with embarrassment as their gazes met her. But then one of the students smiled and beckoned her over.

"Hey there," the girl said, "I'm Kaelin. Welcome to the Academy!"

Elara smiled back, feeling a sense of relief flood through her.

"Elara," she said in a very small voice.

Kaelin looked a little older than Elara, and wore long dark green robes that reached her ankles, just like all the others in the room. It was clearly a uniform and as Elara looked down at her own tattered shirt and trousers, she couldn't help but feel a little jealous.

"Just got here then?" Kaelin asked with a smile.

Elara nodded. "It wasn't easy to find actually… and I only just realised I've got magic inside me…"

Kaelin practically beamed. "That's alright, you won't be judged here! Some of us found the Academy by accident and others were here from the beginning. Either way, we're all in this together, right?"

Elara nodded once. "I just hope I'll learn something to help out around here," she said. "I can't go home anymore and…"

"Don't worry about any of that," Kaelin interrupted. "And your home is right here with us!"

Kaelin seemed to have a way with her words that just put Elara at ease. Normally, she would've shied away from a gathering like whatever this was, but Kaelin had already made her feel comfortable and welcome.

"Where… where did all these people come from?" Elara asked as she scanned the room. It was full of people who seemed as though they didn't have a care in the world. "Did they all escape the city and find their way here?" It was a bit of a long shot, Elara knew, but she couldn't figure out how normal this all seemed to so many people.

Kaelin took a deep breath before she began to explain. "Well, the city isn't as bleak as it seems. Pockets of resistance within the city work to help mages escape the notice of the guard. These people help to ensure their safe passage to the Academy, but they don't leave the city. I don't know where all the mages go, but the ones with green eyes come here, and I know there's a place for the red-eyed fire mages."

Elara listened intently, feeling a glimmer of hope for the first time since her world had been turned upside down. She had always thought that the city was devoid of any kindness or goodness, but Kaelin's words suggested that perhaps there was something more there. To think that there were people working in secret to help others escape the wrath of the Tyrant King Roderick was awe-inspiring.

"And you made it here all on your own?" Kaelin asked, looking at Elara with a mix of surprise and admiration.

Elara nodded, feeling a small sense of pride well up within her. "It wasn't easy, but I managed." She remembered that Darien had told her not to mention him or Mara, and she wasn't about to break that promise.

Kaelin smiled. "Well, you've certainly got a strong will. That's a good thing to have in these trying times. The forest is dangerous though, you shouldn't go out there alone again."

Elara felt a sense of warmth spread through her chest at Kaelin's words. It was nice to feel like she belonged somewhere, even if it was just within the walls of the Academy.

"What about you?" Elara asked, looking around the room. "How did you end up here?"

Kaelin's smile faded slightly, and Elara could sense a hint of sadness in her voice as she spoke. "I was born with my affinity. My family was forced to flee the city when things changed, and we've been on the run ever since. We were lucky enough to stumble upon the Academy a year or so ago, and I've been here ever since."

Elara could hardly imagine what it would be like to be on the run for so long but Kaelin seemed to take it all in stride. She was amazed by the strength and resilience of the people around her and knew that she had a lot to learn from them if she was going to survive in this new world.

"Wait, your parents are here too? Are they mages?" Elara hadn't thought it yet, but if this place offered sanctuary, perhaps her parents could join her too.

Kaelin shook her head solemnly, with a look of sadness on her face. "No, they carried on to find a new place to live. I was offered my place here, but it is only for those with the gift."

"I see," Elara said sadly. "I guess I might see my parents again one day, though." Then a thought occurred to her. "Can we leave?" She asked with wide eyes. "You know, go back into the city to visit? See my parents maybe?"

The look that Kaelin gave Elara was filled with sympathy, but before she could reply, an older boy interrupted her.

"You don't want to get caught at the gates. You'll just get 'open your eyes'," he said in a mocking tone, "and if you're lucky, they'll be the last words you ever hear. Mainly it's 'cos you don't want to get tortured. Despicable things they do to mages back in the city now, I hear."

Elara turned to look at the boy, who had a mischievous glint in his eyes. He was tall and lean, with sandy blonde hair that was tousled in a carefree way. He wore long worn robes as the rest did, but somehow they managed to look cool and effortless on him.

Kaelin rolled her eyes, but there was a hint of fondness in her expression as she addressed the boy.

"This is Rylan. He's one of the seniors here, and he likes to scare the newbies."

Rylan grinned unapologetically. "What can I say? It's my favourite pastime." He turned to Elara and gave her a playful wink. "But seriously. You don't want to go back to the city. It's a dangerous place for mages these days."

Elara couldn't help but feel a little charmed by Rylan's carefree attitude, despite the seriousness of the situation. She had never been around people like him before, people who seemed to take everything in stride and always had a quick comeback.

"Besides," Rylan continued, "you've got everything you need here. Good company, decent food, and a roof over your head. What more could you ask for?"

Elara considered Rylan's words for a moment, realising that he was right. She felt like she was safe here, among people who understood her and accepted her for who she was. It was a feeling that she had never experienced before, and it was both comforting and exhilarating at the same time.

"Thanks, Rylan," Kaelin said with a small smile. "I'll make sure to remember that the next time Elara gets restless."

Rylan chuckled. "Anytime, Kaelin. Anytime." He gave Elara another playful wink before sauntering off, his hands in his pockets.

Elara watched him go, feeling a smile tug at the corners of her lips. She was starting to realise that life at the Academy was perhaps going to be a lot more interesting than she had initially thought.

Chapter 4: Training Begins

"Come oooon, Elara," Kaelin whinged as Elara tried for the hundredth time to will her mana into doing something, anything that would cause some magical effect. "Once you can move your mana around like it's a part of you, you'll be able to learn spells properly! Until then, well… I hate to say this but you kind of look like you need the toilet right now."

Elara hadn't noticed she'd been hopping from foot to foot as she tried her best to control her mana.

The room that they were practising in was more of a chamber. Elara couldn't even see the dirt of the walls through the roots that covered them and again, vibrant green plantlife and colourful flowers covered the walls. The room was empty except for a few other pairs talking quietly and Elara guessed they too were practising.

When Elara had returned to her room to sleep, she'd found that someone had left robes for her to wear, and that they were soft, warm and new. Before she went to sleep, she couldn't help but try them on.

Kaelin had knocked on Elara's door before she had even awoken and it seemed like she was more excited for Elara's first day in training than Elara was.

Elara let out a sigh of frustration as she shook her head at Kaelin. "I'm trying," she said, her voice tinged with annoyance. "It's just not working."

Kaelin rolled her eyes. "I know you're trying," she said. "But you need to focus. Clear your mind and let your mana flow through you."

Elara took a deep breath, closed her eyes, and tried to clear her mind. She imagined her mana as a seed again, growing within her body, but it still refused to cooperate. She opened her eyes and shook her head in defeat.

Kaelin let out a sympathetic sigh. "It's okay," she said."

"Why are you teaching me again? I thought Master Arin would be here."

"You thought the Headmaster would be teaching you one on one? Are you mental?" Kaelin asked. "The journeymen teach the Apprentices, they teach the journeymen and the Archmage teaches the Master . That's Arin's job."

"So how does Master Arin learn new spells?" Elara asked. "And why is he called a Master when he's an Archmage?"

Kaelin smiled. "Does it really matter what he's called? And anyway, he'd be taught by the Grandmaster if he hadn't been killed by Roderick." Then Kaelin peered at Elara, "But enough of this stalling, control your mana or I'll reach down your throat and take it away from you."

Elara frowned, wondering if Kaelin could actually do that, but decided that she must've been joking. And if she wasn't, she didn't really want to know.

"Can I ask you something?" she said.

Kaelin raised an eyebrow. "Sure, what is it?"

"What do you know about that guy, Rylan?" Elara asked, trying her best to sound casual.

Kaelin let out a sigh. "Why do you want to know about him?" she asked.

"I don't know, he just seems... interesting," Elara replied, feeling a little embarrassed.

Kaelin rolled her eyes. "He's trouble, that's what he is," she said. "Always causing problems and with some of the other guys he likes getting into fights. And he's got a temper like you wouldn't believe."

Elara frowned. It didn't sound like the boy she had spoken to before, he seemed so happy and playful. "But... why? What happened to him to make him like that?"

Kaelin hesitated for a moment before sighing. "I don't really know the whole story," she admitted. "But I heard that his family was killed by the king. He was brought here but I think he wanted to stay and fight in the city. I know he wants revenge, but the King and his soldiers are just too powerful. Arin doesn't want him leaving here until he knows how to control himself."

Elara listened quietly, feeling a pang of sympathy for Rylan. She couldn't imagine what it would be like to lose her family like that. At least she was pretty sure they were still alive back in the city.

"Is there anything we can do to help him?" she asked.

Kaelin snorted. "I doubt it," she said. "He's too proud to accept help from anyone. And besides, he's already on thin ice with Arin. If he messes up again, he'll be kicked out for sure."

Elara felt a twinge of disappointment, but she knew Kaelin was probably right. "I see," she said quietly. Then something occurred to her. Was this the reason that Darien and Mara had been out there all alone? Because they'd had a falling out with Master Arin? She knew she couldn't ask the question, but she filed the information away for later.

Kaelin put a hand on her shoulder. "Don't worry about him too much," she said. "He doesn't need your worry. You on the other hand need my pity. So, let's get back to it; I want to see you controlling your mana by the end of the week!"

But Elara couldn't help but wonder if there was something she could do to help Rylan. She made a mental note to keep an eye on him and see if there was anything she could do to make his life a little easier.

As they resumed their training, Elara couldn't shake off the feeling of unease that had settled in her stomach. She didn't know Rylan very well, but she knew what it was like to feel alone and desperate for help. She wondered if there was something she could do, some way she could reach out to him without making things worse.

After their training was over and Elara had remained unable to affect her mana in any tangible way, she decided to take a walk around the Academy to clear her head. As she walked, she found herself drawn towards an open training arena, where the sun shone down from above. It was strange as most of the Academy was underground, but this area seemed to allow both daylight and fresh air to radiate down onto a circular sandpit that was clearly intended for practising in a big way.

Elara's gaze then fell upon the one and only person standing upon the sands: Rylan was practising what looked like sword fighting, alone.

She watched him for a few moments, unsure of what to do or say. She watched as Rylan swung his sword with practised ease in the sandy training arena. She had heard Kaelin's warning about Rylan being too proud to accept help, but she couldn't help but feel drawn to him and as she approached, she couldn't help but ask, "Why do you use a sword when you can do magic?"

Rylan didn't stop his movements, but he answered without looking at her. "Magic isn't always at hand," he said. "A sword is a reliable weapon."

Elara nodded, understanding his point. "But what if you could use both?" she asked. "Wouldn't that be even more powerful?"

Rylan finally turned to face her, his eyes narrowing slightly. "Can you use your magic yet?" he asked sceptically.

Elara sighed, knowing that she still had a lot to learn. "No," she admitted.

"But I'm working on it."

Rylan nodded, seemingly satisfied with her answer. He then walked over to a wall where a variety of swords hung and retrieved one, handing it to Elara. "If you're going to learn, you'll need a weapon," he said.

Elara took the sword, feeling its weight in her hand. She had never held a sword before, but it felt natural in her grip, comfortable even. It didn't seem as though it was very sharp for a sword, though.

Rylan stepped back and readied his own sword, clearly an invitation to spar which Elara accepted, and they began to move around each other in a graceful dance, their swords held up and to the ready.

At first, Elara's movements were awkward and clumsy as she tried to mimic Rylan's stances. But as they continued to move, she began to find her rhythm.

Elara quickly realised that this was much more than just a simple training match with brutish weapons. It was a dance, a beautiful choreography of steel and magic.

Rylan moved with a fluidity that was almost mesmerising, but Elara was determined to keep up. She focused on the weight of the weapon in her hand, and the way Rylan's movements seemed to anticipate her own.

After a long while where neither moved to cause the swords to clash, they eventually both moved with fluid grace, anticipating each other's moves and countering the steps with their own. Elara's sword had started to feel like it was an extension of her body, and she moved with a confidence she had never known before.

When they finally finished, both of them breathing heavily, Elara put her sword back on the wall and walked over to Rylan.

"That was beautiful," he said softly.

Elara smiled, feeling a sense of pride in herself. "Thank you," she said.

Rylan then held his sword out for Elara to take. "This was my father's sword," he said. "He held it as he died, trying to save my family. When I'm holding it, I feel a connection to them. I don't know if it really does hold some power within, but it makes me feel at peace."

Elara took the sword, feeling the weight of Rylan's past in her hand. She knew that she had just witnessed something special between them, something that went beyond words. She silently vowed to do whatever she could to help Rylan in his quest for revenge.

"Actually, you know…" Elara said with a crooked smile. "I thought by the way you trained you'd be better with a sword, I mean you didn't hit me once!"

Rylan looked fake hurt for just a second before announcing: "Oh you want a real match do you?"

Elara and Rylan sat down on the sand after their training bouts, catching their breaths. Elara didn't think she had worked this hard in her entire life. She hadn't hit Rylan once, not even come close and on no less than twenty occasions, he had tapped her with his sword.

Elara was the first to break the silence, her voice quiet and uncertain.

"I'm worried I'll never be able to control my mana,' she said, her eyes downcast. "I couldn't seem to do anything in training with Kaelin today."

Rylan turned to her, his expression sympathetic. "Don't worry about that," he said. "Everyone is different. The mana within you is an extension of yourself. You just need to find your own way of shaping it. The learning really comes after that."

Elara looked up at him, her eyes wide with surprise. 'How do you shape your mana?" she asked.

Rylan smiled, his eyes glinting with a sense of pride. "For me, it's like a mighty oak that fills my body," he said. "I can call on the limbs of the tree to create my spells."

Elara looked at him in wonder, but then she shook her head. "I don't see my mana like that," she said.

"When I put my hand on the door, it was like a seed, right there in my heart. I tried to make it move around like Kaelin was saying but it just wouldn't budge. Do you think it's broken?"

Rylan shook his head. "It takes time to figure it out," he said. "But once you do, it'll be like second nature to you."

Elara sighed, feeling frustrated with herself. "But what if I can't figure it out?" she asked. "What if I'm just not cut out for magic?'

Rylan placed a comforting hand on her shoulder. "That's not true," he said firmly. "Everyone has their own strengths and weaknesses. You just need to keep practising and experimenting. And don't be too hard on yourself. It'll happen for you just like it's happened to everyone else here."

Elara looked at him gratefully, feeling a sense of comfort in his words. "Thank you," she said softly. Then she realised what he had said and added: "Everyone else? You're saying I'm the only Apprentice here? The only one who can't do any spells?"

Rylan smiled at her, a warmth in his eyes, but didn't answer her question.

"You know, I'm a Master rank," he said, almost casually.

Elara's eyes widened in surprise. "Really?" she said. "That's amazing. How long did it take you to get there?"

Rylan shrugged. "A few years," he said. "But it's not about how long it takes. It's about the journey. And the things you learn along the way."

Elara nodded, feeling inspired by his words. She knew that she still had a long way to go, but with Rylan's guidance and support, she felt more confident than ever that she could achieve her goals. She couldn't believe that he was a Master rank too, where she thought he was just above her on the scales, he was two ranks above.

Rylan reached into a small pouch at his waist and pulled out a delicate silver locket. It was intricately crafted, with delicate filigree patterns etched onto its surface. The locket was small enough to fit in the palm of his hand, and Elara peered down at it with interest.

"Here," he said, holding it out to Elara. "Take this. It was how I practised my mana at first. If you focus, you can unlock it."

Elara took the locket from him, her fingers brushing against the cool metal. She examined it closely, taking in the delicate details etched into the surface.

"It's beautiful," she said softly, before looking up at Rylan with a grateful smile. "But how do I do it?"

Rylan nodded, his expression serious. "It's more than just a piece of jewellery," he said. "It's a tool. If you can focus your mana and unlock the locket, you'll be one step closer to mastering your abilities. But I can't tell you how. Your control over your mana will dictate that."

Elara nodded, tucking the locket safely into her pocket. She felt a sense of determination welling up inside of her. She was going to Master her mana, no matter what it took.

"Thank you, Rylan," she said, looking up at him with sincerity in her eyes. "I won't let you down."

Rylan simply nodded in response, his expression unreadable. Then he stood up, turned and walked away, leaving Elara alone with her thoughts and the weight of the locket firmly in her pocket.

Chapter 5: From the Smallest Seed

It was the next morning and the sun shone brightly in the sky, casting a warm glow over the courtyard where the breakfast feast was being held. The long wooden tables were covered with crisp white tablecloths and adorned with colourful floral centrepieces. The smell of freshly baked bread and steaming hot porridge filled the air, and people bustled about, carrying platters of fruit and vegetable dishes to the tables.

It was the first time that Elara had the chance to see how many people called the Academy their home. Almost everyone wore matching robes and not many of the mages looked over thirty.

Kaelin and Elara sat at a table near the edge of the courtyard, overlooking the lush green gardens beyond with no sign of the terrible Forbidden Forest anywhere to be seen. Kaelin took a bite of her grilled mushrooms and looked over at Elara, who seemed lost in thought.

"What's on your mind, Elara?" Kaelin asked.

Elara sighed. "It's Rylan again," she said. "I just can't seem to get a handle on my mana like he can. He makes it sound so easy, like he's been doing it his whole life."

Kaelin nodded sympathetically. "Rylan is a Master ranked mage, Elara. It's no surprise he's so skilled with his mana. But that doesn't mean you can't be just as skilled in your own way."

"I know," Elara said, pushing her porridge around her bowl with her spoon. "But I'm worried I'll never be able to control my mana like I want to. And if I can't, what kind of mage will I be?"

Kaelin placed a comforting hand on Elara's arm. "You'll be the kind of mage you're meant to be, Elara. And that's something to be proud of, no matter what."

Elara managed a small smile. "Thanks, Kaelin. You always know just what to say."

As they continued their breakfast, the talk around them turned to the possibility of Archmage Arin being able to control the weather, giving them the beautiful sunlight that currently warmed them all. Some speculated that it was his powerful mana at work, while others simply enjoyed the warm and sunny morning.

Desperate to think about anything else, Elara turned to Kaelin and asked, "Hey, Kaelin, have you noticed that we can't see the forest from here?"

Kaelin looked up from her plate, following Elara's gaze. "Yeah, I guess that is strange," she replied. "But I heard that the forest is enchanted. Maybe that has something to do with it?"

Elara raised her eyebrows. "Enchanted? What do you mean?"

"I don't know," Kaelin shrugged. "I overheard some of the senior students talking about it. They said that the forest is home to some powerful magic, and that it's been enchanted to keep outsiders away. But then it could all just be an illusion to keep us hidden from the soldiers, right?"

Elara furrowed her brow, deep in thought. She had never heard of an enchanted forest before, but it made sense. After all, the Academy was surely home to some of the most powerful mages in the land, and it was only natural that they would want to protect their secrets.

As the conversation drifted to other topics, Elara couldn't shake the feeling that there was more to the forest than met the eye. She made a mental note to ask Rylan about it later, hoping he would have some answers.

The meal ended with workers clearing away the dishes and the mages heading off to their daily lessons and training. Elara couldn't shake the feeling of inadequacy that had settled over her, but Kaelin's words had given her a glimmer of hope. Maybe one day she would be able to control her mana like Rylan, in her own way.

Once the pair had finished their breakfast, they then walked back into the Academy proper, ready to spend some more time training with their mana. Of course, Kaelin would need to do her own training at some point, but it seemed until Elara gained at least a small amount of control over her mana, this was the direction that the pair was going to take. Elara was eternally grateful for the help that she was getting though.

Kaelin and Elara made their way back to the Academy, walking through the underground tunnel that led from the courtyard to the main entrance. The dimly lit corridor was cool and damp, a stark contrast to the warm sunlight they had just left behind. The walls were made of rough-hewn stone, and the floor was uneven and covered in patches of moss and lichen. The only sound was the echo of their footsteps as they walked. Within a few moments, they had reached the cavern where Elara had already once attempted to gain control over her mana.

Elara sat cross-legged on the ground, her eyes closed in deep concentration. She had been trying to work with her mana all morning, but nothing seemed to be working. She couldn't help but feel frustrated and discouraged. She knew that she had a long way to go before she could control her mana like Rylan, but she couldn't even seem to get started.

"Who's your teacher anyway?" Elara asked, her eyes snapping open.

Kaelin, who was standing nearby, watching Elara whilst absent-mindedly tapping her foot on the ground smiled.

Kaelin replied, "My teacher's name is Anya. She's tough, but she knows her stuff. She's been helping me with my mana control and elemental manipulation for the past few months, and I've learned a lot from her."

Elara nodded, impressed. She hadn't heard of Master Anya before, or come to think about it any of the other journeymen or Master really.

It made Elara wonder if Kaelin's progress was a result of her teacher's expertise or her own hard work and determination.

"Well, I'm glad you have a good teacher," Elara said, smiling at her friend. "Maybe someday I'll be lucky enough to have a Master like that. You know, someone who actually helps me." She threw Kaelin a sarcastic smile and Kaelin let out a snort.

"I'm sure you will. You're already making progress, Elara. I can see it. You're almost there, I promise it'll all make sense soon."

Elara took a deep breath and tried to clear her mind again as she closed her eyes, focusing only on the feeling of her mana inside her. It still felt like a tiny seed, buried deep within her heart. She could feel it there, a small, barely perceptible presence.

She thought of Rylan's mana, which he said was like a towering oak tree, strong and powerful. She knew that she could never match his strength, but she didn't have to. She could be her own kind of mage, with her own strengths and abilities and then something occurred to her. Her mana wasn't like a mighty oak tree. It was a seed, and from her time working the land with her parents, she knew that seeds could not be forced into growth, they needed to be nurtured, allowed the space and time to grow at their own pace.

Elara opened her eyes, feeling a sense of renewed energy and purpose. She knew that she had a lot of work to do, but for the first time, she felt like she had a plan. She would tend to her seed, nurture it, and watch it grow.

With new determination she concentrated and then she began to feel something stirring within her. It was like tiny tendrils were sprouting from the seed, searching for room to grow. She focused all of her attention on these tiny tendrils, willing them to grow stronger but also comforting them so that they knew it was safe to emerge.

Slowly, she began to feel a sense of warmth spreading through her body, as if the tendrils were reaching out and touching every part of her being. It was a small sensation, and the tendrils were thin and weak, but it was enough to give her hope. She realised now that as her mana was like a seed, she was like its gardener. She had to nurture it, help it grow and not try to force it to move.

Kaelin watched in amazement as Elara's mana began to stir. She could feel the energy radiating from her friend and knew that something significant was happening.

"That's it, Elara," Kaelin whispered, not wanting to break her friend's concentration. "You've got this."

Elara's breathing became slow and steady as she continued to focus on the tiny tendrils of her mana. She felt a sense of peace wash over her, as if she were in a garden, surrounded by the soft rustle of leaves and the gentle trickle of water.

She continued to nurture her mana, willing it to grow, but not forcing it. She knew that it would take time and patience, but she was willing to put in the work.

After what felt like an eternity, Elara opened her eyes. Kaelin could see a sense of wonder and amazement in them.

"I did it," Elara whispered. "I actually did it."

Kaelin smiled, feeling a sense of pride for her friend. "You did it, Elara. And you'll do it again. And again. Until it becomes second nature."

Elara nodded, still feeling the warmth of her mana within her. She knew that she had a long journey ahead of her, but for the first time, she felt like it was possible.

"Thank you, Kaelin," she said, turning to her friend. "I couldn't have done it without you."

Kaelin shrugged, feeling a sense of humility. "I just helped you along the way. The rest was all you."

Elara smiled, feeling a sense of gratitude towards her friend. With Kaelin by her side, she felt like anything was possible.

Then as if from nowhere, Rylan entered the chamber and his eyes fell upon the two girls in practice.

Seeing the determined expression on Elara's face. He raised an eyebrow, intrigued, and turned to Kaelin. "Well, well, well, looks like Elara's finally getting the hang of this magic stuff. Must be all those hours of practice paying off," he said, his tone dripping with sarcasm.

Kaelin rolled her eyes and shot Rylan a playful glare. "Give her a break, Rylan. She's doing her best, and she's come a long way since she started."

Rylan shrugged. "Hey, I'm just calling it like I see it. And right now, I see someone who's starting to look like a real mage."

Elara couldn't help but smile at Rylan's words, despite his teasing tone. She knew he had a knack for making fun of people, but there was always a hint of kindness hidden beneath his sarcasm. "Thanks, Rylan. I appreciate it," she said, feeling a warmth spread through her chest.

Rylan grinned back at her, a mischievous glint in his eye. "Don't get too excited though, you still have a long way to go before you catch up to me."

Elara rolled her eyes, but she couldn't deny the feeling of happiness that Rylan's compliment had given her. She was grateful for his encouragement, even if he did have a funny way of showing it.

Elara felt her cheeks grow warm at Rylan's compliment, but she quickly composed herself and said, "Thanks, Rylan. You're always so charming." She couldn't resist teasing him back.

Rylan grinned. "I try my best. So, what are you guys up to?"

"We're just practising our mana control," Kaelin replied.

Rylan raised an eyebrow. "Really? How's that going for you?"

Kaelin rolled her eyes. "It's going fine, thanks for asking."

Elara spoke up, wanting to show Rylan that she was making progress too. "Actually, I'm starting to feel something," she said, a note of excitement in her voice.

Rylan's eyes shone a deep green. "Really? That's great, Elara! What are you feeling?"

Elara hesitated, not wanting to sound foolish, but Kaelin gave her an encouraging nod. "It's hard to describe, but it's like I can feel my mana starting to grow. It's still small, but it's there."

Rylan nodded. "That's amazing, Elara. Keep at it and soon you could have a powerful oak tree like mine," he said with a wink. "By the way have you managed to open my locket yet?"

"Giving the new girl jewellery already Rylan? I should've known," Kaelin said with a snort.

"No…" Elara said slowly, ignoring Kaelin. "I'll keep trying and I think it might be easier now that I can feel the mana inside me properly."

"Just keep trying," Rylan said with a genuine smile. "You'll get it soon enough."

What Elara didn't want to say, was that she had been trying to open the locket all night. She wanted so much to impress Rylan by opening the thing and had reached a point where she was just about ready to smash the thing open on the floor but had thought better of it. With her new control over mana though, she wondered if her next attempt would be somehow different.

Kaelin rolled her eyes at the two of them, but secretly, she was happy to see Elara making progress. She knew how important it was to her new friend to prove herself and show that she was capable of mastering her magic. And with Rylan's support, Kaelin was sure that Elara would succeed.

"So, Rylan, what brings you here?" Kaelin asked, changing the subject.

Rylan shrugged. "Just passing by. I thought I'd drop in and see what you guys were up to," he replied nonchalantly.

Kaelin raised an eyebrow. "Uh-huh. And what else?"

Rylan smirked. "Okay, fine. I also wanted to see if Elara had managed to control her mana yet," he admitted.

Kaelin raised an eyebrow. "You're impossible, Rylan."

Rylan grinned. "That's what they tell me."

Elara couldn't help but laugh at Rylan's response. Despite his teasing and sarcastic nature, she found herself enjoying his company. There was something about him that made her feel comfortable and at ease, even when he was being difficult.

"Well, thanks for checking in on me," Elara said.

Rylan grinned. "Hey, that's what friends are for right? And speaking of friends, I think it's time we introduce Elara to some more of ours."

Elara's heart skipped a beat. She had never been very good at making friends, and the thought of meeting more people was a little intimidating. But she trusted Rylan and knew that he wouldn't lead her astray.

"Sure, I'd love to meet more of your friends," she said, trying to sound confident.

Kaelin smiled at Elara. "Don't worry, you'll love them. They're a pretty great bunch," she said reassuringly.

Rylan clapped his hands together. "Alright then, let's go. I'll introduce you to the gang." He turned to Elara with a mischievous grin. "But be warned, they can be a little... unpredictable." Elara laughed, feeling her nerves dissipate. She had a feeling that this was going to be anything but boring, at least.

Chapter 6: Growth

As they walked through the halls of the Academy and into another chamber that was furnished with tables and chair with groups of people sat all around, Rylan and Kaelin beckoned Elara to join a table with a boy and a girl sat facing each other.

"This is Landon," Rylan said, gesturing to a tall, dark muscular boy with brown hair. "He's one of the strongest Master I know."

Landon nodded in greeting, his expression serious. "Nice to meet you, Elara. Rylan's told us all about you."

"And this is Anya," Rylan said, indicating a petite girl with bright green eyes. "She's OK, you'll get used to her I guess."

Anya smiled warmly at Elara then scowled at Rylan.

Elara smiled back, feeling a sense of belonging for the first time in a long while. These people were like her, and she knew that they would understand the struggles she faced as a new mage.

Kaelin pulled out a chair for Elara, and she sat down gratefully, glancing around the table at her new friends. "Thank you for welcoming me," she said sincerely.

Landon leaned forward, his expression intense. "So, Rylan tells us you've been working on your mana control. How's it going?"

Elara hesitated, not wanting to admit her lack of progress, but then decided to be honest. "I'm still struggling, but I'm determined to get better," she said, looking down at her hands.

Anya spoke up, her voice playful. "Don't worry, we'll whip you into shape in no time. And if all else fails, we'll just hit Rylan up for some of his secret training techniques."

Rylan groaned, but couldn't help but laugh at Anya's comment. "Hey, I'm not the only one with tricks up my sleeve," he said, nudging Kaelin.

Kaelin rolled her eyes but smiled fondly at Rylan. "We'll all help you, Elara. And who knows, maybe we'll even learn something from you," she said, her eyes twinkling mischievously.

Elara smiled back, feeling a sense of hope and excitement for the first time since she arrived at the Academy. These were her people, and she knew that with their help, she could achieve anything.

As Elara settled into her seat at the table, she watched as Rylan, Landon, and Anya exchanged playful banter. They joked and teased each other, their easy camaraderie evident to anyone who watched them.

"You know, Rylan, you really need to work on your elemental summoning," Anya said with a smirk. "I mean, you can barely summon a pebble these days."

Rylan rolled his eyes. "Yeah, well at least I don't waste my mana on useless tricks like turning flowers into gold."

Anya laughed. "Hey, it's not useless if you can sell the gold for a profit."

Landon chimed in, "Well, I don't know about you two, but I'm still trying to figure out how to make a rock levitate without it dropping on my head."

Elara couldn't help but smile at their banter. It was clear that they were all close friends who shared a love of magic and a willingness to poke fun at each other.

"And what about you, Elara?" Landon asked, turning to her. "What's your specialty?"

Elara shifted in her seat, feeling a bit self-conscious. "I'm still trying to Master the basics, to be honest. I'm working on my mana control right now."

Rylan nudged her with his elbow. "Don't worry about it. We've all been there."

Anya nodded. "Yeah, we were all clueless newbies at one point. You'll get the hang of it."

As the banter continued between Rylan, Landon, and Anya, Kaelin pulled Elara aside and whispered, "I've never been offered to sit with the Master before. I don't know what you've got over Rylan, but you're something different, Elara."

Elara felt a surge of pride and happiness. She had never felt so welcomed and accepted before. "Thank you," she replied, smiling at Kaelin. But also, she wondered exactly what Rylan's game was, and why he would even show her the smallest amount of interest.

"I'm serious," Kaelin said. "You have a gift, and they can see that. Don't let anyone tell you otherwise."

Elara nodded, feeling grateful for Kaelin's encouragement. She had always doubted herself and her abilities, but Kaelin's words gave her a newfound confidence. "I won't," she promised.

Kaelin smiled. "Good. You have a lot of potential, Elara. I can't wait to see what you can do."

Elara grinned and turned back to the three Master , and one Journeyman mage sat around the table.

"So where should I start?" Elara asked.

Rylan smirked at her. "Well, you could start by trying to open my locket. I mean, you seem to be obsessed with it."

Elara rolled her eyes but couldn't help but feel a pang of disappointment. She had been hoping that Rylan had forgotten about the locket and would give her some actual advice.

Landon chuckled. "Don't worry, Elara. Rylan's just teasing. We can help you with your mana control. It's important to have a good foundation before you move on to more advanced spells."

Anya nodded enthusiastically. "Yeah, and I can help you with your elemental manipulation when you've got the hang of things. It's all about understanding the properties of your mana and how it interacts with things."

Elara felt a surge of gratitude towards her new friends. They were willing to help her, even though she was just a beginner. "Thank you," she said sincerely. "I really appreciate it."

Rylan grinned. "Of course, we're a team here. We all help each other out." Elara couldn't help but smile back at him. Maybe Rylan wasn't so bad after all. She was beginning to see that he had a playful and caring side, even if he did have a tendency to tease her.

As Elara thanked the others for their willingness to help, Kaelin spoke up. "I can help too, if you want. I'm not as experienced as these guys, but I've some experience with mana manipulation and control."

Elara turned to Kaelin, surprised but pleased. "I know you'll be great, and thankyou again," she said.

Rylan raised an eyebrow. "Well, look at you, Kaelin. You're becoming quite the expert yourself."

Kaelin shrugged. "I have a lot of free time these days," she said with a grin.

Landon chimed in. "We could all use more practice with mana control. It's the foundation of everything we do."

Anya nodded. "Exactly. And we can all learn from each other."

Elara felt a warmth in her chest at the inclusiveness of the group. They were all willing to help each other, regardless of their experience levels. It was a refreshing change from the competitiveness and elitism that she had experienced in the past.

"Thank you all," she said, feeling grateful for her new friends. "I can't wait to learn from you."

Kaelin smiled at Elara. "We're all in this together. And who knows, maybe we'll discover something new and exciting along the way."

Rylan smirked. "Yeah, like how to turn Landon's hair green again," he joked.

Landon rolled his eyes. "Ha ha, very funny," he said, but couldn't help but grin.

Anya chuckled. "Let's stay focused, shall we? We have a lot of work to do if we want to become the best mages we can be. And you have some catching up to do," she said to Elara.

Elara nodded in agreement. "Yes, let's get started."

"So what does your mana feel like?" Anya asked Elara.

"It uh… it feels like a tiny seed within my heart. I think I can coax it into growing, but if I try to move it too quickly or to force it, it shrinks right back down into the seed."

Landon then said: "My mana feels like a river, constantly flowing and shifting. To control it, I imagine myself as an immovable rock in the middle of the river, letting the mana flow around me but not disturbing my core. When I want to control it, I change the shape of the rock and of the riverbed and that's how I get my mana to where it needs to be."

Anya added: "For me, my mana feels like the roots of a tree, strong and deep. I picture myself as the trunk of the tree, grounded and steady, and let my mana flow through me like the lifeforce through the tree."

Kaelin chimed in next. "My mana feels like a field of flowers, each one different and delicate. To control it, I focus on each flower individually and then weave them together like a tapestry."

Rylan snorted. "My mana feels like a mighty oak tree, resistant to change and set in its ways. I force it to grow within me and when it does, I use the branches to enact my will."

Elara listened to each of them, fascinated by how different their experiences were despite all being earth mages. She took mental notes on their techniques for controlling their mana, hoping to incorporate them into her own practice, but she had the feeling that each person would have to come up with their own way of control.

"I think that I need to treat the seed as though I would on a farm. It needs nurturing rather than force to grow…" Elara said.

Anya nodded in agreement. "That's a great way to think about it. Nurturing your mana will allow it to grow strong and healthy. It takes time and patience, but it's worth it in the end."

Landon added, "And remember, just like with farming, sometimes things don't go according to plan. It's important to be adaptable and adjust your approach when needed."

Rylan smirked. "And sometimes you have to be willing to get your hands dirty."

Kaelin laughed. "I think Elara will be just fine. She's a quick learner and already has a good handle on her mana." Elara smiled, feeling encouraged by their words. She was grateful for their support and guidance.

Anya grinned mischievously. "Well, it looks like Elara is going to teach us all a thing or two about nurturing, Landon. Maybe you should take some notes."

Landon chuckled. "Ha, very funny, Anya. I'll stick to my river analogies, thank you very much."

Rylan chimed in. "And I'll stick to my mighty oak tree. It's served me well so far."

Kaelin rolled her eyes. "I'll leave the farming analogies to Elara. I think I'll stick to my tapestry of flowers."

Elara couldn't help but laugh. It felt good to be a part of a group that could joke around and have fun with each other.

"Well, I think we can all agree that we have different approaches to our mana, but as long as it works for us, that's what matters."

"Agreed," Anya said, smiling. "Now let's get back to work. We have a lot of practicing to do."

Anya nodded. "Okay, Elara. Let's start with the basics. Close your eyes and take a deep breath. Focus on your seed within and imagine it as a small plant. See it sprouting a tiny stem and a pair of leaves."

Elara followed Anya's instructions and visualised the seed growing. At first, nothing happened, but then she felt a faint stirring within her chest. She concentrated harder, willing the seed to grow, and suddenly she felt a small shoot emerge from the seed.

Anya smiled encouragingly. "Good job, Elara. Now imagine roots growing from the stem and reaching down into the earth, anchoring the plant and drawing in nutrients."

Elara concentrated again, and soon she could feel the roots taking shape in her mind's eye. She imagined them digging into the earth, spreading out and seeking nourishment.

Anya nodded in approval. "Excellent, Elara. Now picture the plant growing taller and stronger, reaching for the sky and soaking up the sunlight."

Elara followed Anya's instructions, and to her amazement, she felt the plant growing taller and thicker, its leaves reaching out and turning towards the imaginary sun in her mind. She felt a sense of pride and accomplishment at the sight of her tiny plant thriving.

"Wow, I did it!" she exclaimed, opening her eyes to see the others smiling at her. "Thank you, Anya. I never thought I could do that."

Anya chuckled. "You're a natural, Elara. With some practice, you'll be growing entire gardens in no time." The others laughed and each of them nodded, and Elara felt a warm sense of belonging in the group.

Anya smiled encouragingly at Elara. "Remember to be patient and gentle," she said. "You're coaxing growth from a seed, not forcing it. It takes time and nurturing."

Elara nodded, taking a deep breath and closing her eyes. She focused on the seed within her, picturing it in her mind's eye. She imagined it as a tiny sprout, with delicate leaves and a fragile stem. She pictured herself as a caretaker, tending to the sprout with care and attention.

Slowly, she began to draw on her mana, imagining it flowing into the seed like water into soil. She felt a warmth in her chest, a flicker of life within the seed. She focused on that warmth, nurturing it with every breath.

Anya watched closely, offering gentle guidance and encouragement. "That's it, Elara. Keep focusing on the seed. Let the mana flow into it, and let it grow at its own pace."

For what felt like hours, Elara remained in that state, completely focused on the tiny sprout within her. She felt the warmth within it growing, the stem thickening and the leaves unfurling. It was a slow process, but she was determined to see it through.

And then it was gone. The sapling wilted and browned, then retreated back into the seed and sat unmoving.

Anya placed a comforting hand on Elara's shoulder. "It's okay, Elara. This is just the first step. It takes time and practice to Master the art of nurturing mana. Don't get discouraged."

Elara let out a frustrated sigh. "I know, but I thought I was making progress."

"You were," Anya reassured her. "You felt the seed sprout and grow. That's a huge step forward. Now you just need to keep practising and refining your technique."

Elara nodded, determined not to give up. She knew it would take time, but she was willing to put in the effort to Master her mana. She took another deep breath and closed her eyes once more, ready to try again.

Chapter 7: The Hunt

Elara lay on her bed, staring up at the ceiling. She absentmindedly twisted the locket in her hands, lost in thought. She had been working hard to cultivate her mana, but she still struggled to control it fully. It was like trying to coax a scared animal into trusting her, scarpering at the last moment just when she thought she had it.

But she had been working so hard, and she could feel that the control over her mana was within her grasp. As she lay there, she felt a strange sensation in her fingertips. It was like a tingling warmth, spreading through her hands and up her arms. She sat up, feeling a surge of excitement. Was this what it felt like to have a better control over her mana?

She closed her eyes and focused, drawing on her mana and coaxing it to flow down her arms and into her fingertips. It was like dipping her fingers into a pool of liquid warmth, and she felt the tendrils of mana weaving through her skin and muscle. She felt the seed grow again, the roots breaking free to draw in the goodness that she fed into it. She felt the shoot rising from its top and the leaves beginning to unfold as her mana grew.

With a surge of confidence, Elara focused on the locket in her hand. She imagined the tendrils of mana flowing into the lock, coaxing it to open. She could feel the resistance, like a locked door that refused to budge, but she pressed on.

But no matter how hard she tried, the lock remained stubbornly closed. The tendrils of mana flickered and faded, leaving her feeling frustrated and defeated.

Elara let out a sigh and collapsed back onto her bed, the locket still held tightly in her hand. She knew she still had a long way to go in mastering her mana, but for now, she just needed to rest and regroup. She closed her eyes and let her mind drift, dreaming of the day when she would finally unlock the secrets of her mana.

But her rest was short-lived. A loud knock on her door startled her out of her reverie. Elara sat up, wondering who could be visiting her at this hour. She quickly composed herself and called out, "Who is it?"

"It's Kaelin," came the reply, her voice urgent. "We need to talk."

Elara felt a knot form in her stomach. Her friend's tone was serious, and she couldn't help but wonder what could be so urgent. She got up from her bed and hurried to the door, opening it to reveal a worried-looking Kaelin.

"What's wrong?" Elara asked, feeling a sense of dread creeping up on her.

"It's the soldiers," Kaelin said, her voice tense. "They're close by, like they know where we could be hiding. They never come this far into the forest and to be near us now..."

Elara felt a surge of fear. She had never been in a situation like this before, and the thought of danger looming so close made her heart race.

"How could they find us? And isn't the forest too dangerous for them?" she asked, her voice trembling slightly.

"We're not sure," Kaelin admitted. "But we need to be prepared for anything. We need to gather together with the rest of the mages in the centre of the Academy so we can keep each other safe and quiet. If they find this place and tell the others… I don't know what'll happen."

Elara nodded, feeling a sense of determination settle over her. She may be scared, but she was also ready to face whatever lay ahead. She quickly followed Kaelin out of the door, steeling herself for the unknown danger that awaited them.

Elara and Kaelin quickly made their way to the centre of the Academy, where the other mages were gathering to discuss what to do about the soldiers. The atmosphere was tense, and Elara could feel the fear and anxiety emanating from the others.

There were so many of them too, more than Elara had ever realised called the hidden Academy their home.

As they joined the group, Elara noticed Rylan standing to the side, his face set in a hard expression. She had never seen him like this before, and she couldn't help but wonder what was going on.

"Rylan, what's wrong?" she asked, walking up to him and placing a hand on his shoulder.

Rylan turned to her, his eyes blazing bright green with anger. "Those soldiers," he spat. "They're the reason my parents are dead. I've been waiting for this moment for years. I want revenge."

Elara felt a chill run down her spine. She had heard about Rylan's tragic past before, but she had never seen him so consumed by his desire for revenge. She had never seen this look in his eye.

"Rylan, revenge isn't the answer," Elara said gently. "We need to stick together and find a way to keep each other safe." She knew that she needed to talk him down from this ledge, but she had no experience in doing so and the boy looked so set on what he wanted to do.

Rylan shook his head, his jaw clenched. "I can't just sit here and do nothing," he said. "I need to take action. It's a few soldiers, sent here to scout for us. I don't know how they know where to look but if we leave any of them alive, they'll come back with an army. I can't let that happen, I won't."

Elara watched as Rylan walked away, his shoulders tense with anger. She couldn't help but feel a sense of worry for him. She knew how destructive the desire for revenge could be, and she didn't want Rylan to do anything that he would regret.

"Rylan! Stop right there!" Master Arin's voice carried across the great hall and Rylan stopped in his tracks. "This is not the way we do things here. We will wait until the soldiers pass and they will know nothing more."

Rylan turned on his heels, and Elara couldn't help but notice that his already stern expression had grown even harder.

Rylan looked across the hall at the Headmaster, his eyes blazing with determination. "I'm going to take out those soldiers," he said. "I'm going to make them pay for what they did to my parents."

Elara felt a surge of fear and sadness wash over her. She knew she needed to stop Rylan before it was too late.

"Rylan, please," she pleaded. "This isn't the answer. We need to find a peaceful solution."

"Rylan, listen to me," she said, her voice soft but firm. "I know how much you're hurting, but this isn't the way. We need to find a peaceful solution, not resort to violence."

Rylan looked at her for a long moment, his eyes searching hers. And then, slowly, he turned and walked from the hall.

"Master?" Elara called to Arin as she ran over to him. "You can't just let him go out there! What about the Academy, the soldiers will know we're here!"

Master Arin didn't meet Elara's gaze as he watched Rylan walking away and Elara had to tap him on the arm to gain his attention. Eventually, Master Arin looked down at Elara and gave her a sad smile.

"I suspect the soldiers have been given a tip as to our location, but if they find Rylan alone in the forest, they will know they are mistaken."

Elara simply couldn't believe what she was hearing. This was not the answer that a caring Headmaster would give.

"I don't understand…" Elara said slowly. "Surely you have to do something… You can't just stand there and let Rylan face those soldiers…"

"Rylan is free to make his choices as he will. And I must place the safety of all of us above the actions of one Master ranked mage."

Then Elara had a thought. "I need to speak to you, Master," she said. "But not here."

Arin looked confused for a moment, then nodded once and stepped out of the hall and into an adjoining tunnel.

"Yes Elara, what can I help you with?" he asked. Ummm… It's not just Rylan out there," she said. She knew that she'd made a promise to the pair who'd helped her find the Academy, but the thought of them alone out there whilst the soldiers were searching for mages made her worried.

The Headmaster looked confused for a second before asking Elara to continue.

"Two people, mages I guess…" Elara said slowly, feeling her betrayal as the words came out. "Darien and Mara… They're out there and if the soldiers find them too…"

Master Arin stroked his beard slowly as he thought. Then finally said: "I do not think there is anything that we can do to help them…"

Elara knew exactly what was coming next and turned to chase after Rylan through the tunnel he had left in. Elara heard Kaelin call out after her as she ran, but she didn't stop for a moment, focussed on doing whatever she could to help Rylan.

As Elara ran through the forest, following Rylan's trail, she felt a sense of unease growing within her. She didn't know what she would find when she caught up with him, but she had a feeling that it wouldn't be good.

Her mind wandered back to the beasts and creatures that she had been told called the Forbidden Forest their home, and hoped more than anything that they wouldn't make their presences known.

Finally, after what felt like an eternity and after her heart was beating faster than she'd ever thought possible, Elara spotted a clearing ahead of her. She slowed her pace and crept forward, trying to stay hidden behind the trees.

As she approached the edge of the clearing, she could see that there was a large pit in the centre of it, and as she crept forward, there, lying on the floor of the pit, was Rylan, unconscious. He was so far down, further than Elara could reach.

She tried calling down to Rylan to rouse him while keeping her anxious voice somewhere between a scared whisper and a shout, but it was no use. She lay on her front and reached down as far as she could, but the distance was simply too much.

Then something dawned on her. If this trap had been set by the soldiers as they searched for the Academy, finding Rylan here like this and in his Academy robes no less, would mean their suspicions were well founded, and more would come.

Elara began to panic. She didn't know what to do next. She knew she couldn't fight the soldiers if they came but equally, she knew she couldn't just leave Rylan there to be captured. Something that above all else would probably lead to the eventual downfall of the entire Academy.

Elara took a deep breath, trying to calm herself down and think rationally. She knew she had to get Rylan out of that pit, but how? She looked around, trying to find something she could use to reach him. But all she saw were trees and bushes. Then she remembered the mana weaving lessons she had learned at the Academy. She had never been very good at it, but it was worth a try.

Elara closed her eyes and focused all her energy on her hands. She pictured the mana flowing through her veins, gathering at her fingertips, and then extending outwards in tendrils. Slowly, she felt the mana respond to her will, and she opened her eyes to see thin, wispy strands of green light emanating from her palms.

She smiled to herself in disbelief, then concentrated all of her attention on her mana. She knew that she couldn't try to force it as it would withdraw from her again. But she could feel the limits of her will as the mana ebbed and flowed with her intent.

Elara extended her arms over the pit and willed the tendrils to reach down and wrap around Rylan. She begged them to comply and at first, it didn't seem to be working, but then she felt the mana obey her will, and she knew she could do this.

As she concentrated, the tendrils began to glow brighter, and she felt them reach and tighten around Rylan's body. The mana began to lift him slowly, Elara's heart pounding in her chest, and then she felt Rylan was in the air before her and finally free of the pit.

Elara collapsed onto the ground, her chest heaving with exhaustion, but also relief. She had done it. Rylan was safe, his body lay on the dirt next to her, and they could get out of sight before the soldiers arrived. She looked up at Rylan, who was still unconscious, but breathing steadily. She smiled weakly, trying to figure out how to get away from this place and back to the

Academy.

But then she remembered Darien and Mara.

Elara's heart sank as she realised that Darien and Mara were still out there somewhere, possibly in danger. She knew she couldn't leave them behind, but she also couldn't carry Rylan and search for them at the same time. She needed a plan, and fast.

Elara sat up, taking deep breaths to clear her mind. She looked around, trying to think of a solution.

As Rylan opened his eyes and groaned, Elara let out a sigh of relief. "Thank goodness you're okay," she said, helping him sit up. "I was so worried when I found you in that pit."

Rylan rubbed his head, still a little dazed. "What happened?"

"I don't know," Elara said, "but we need to get out of here before the soldiers come back. How could you be so stupid to go out there on your own?"

Rylan nodded, looking around. "Do you know the way back to the Academy?" he asked, ignoring Elara's admonishment.

Elara shook her head. "I'm not sure. But first, there's something I need to tell you." She took a deep breath and recounted everything that had happened before the Academy with Darien and Mara. "We need to find them," she said. "They're out there alone and if soldiers are searching the forest for mages…"

Rylan nodded solemnly. "I don't think we have the time to try to find them, and I don't want you out here in danger. I'll send up a warning," he said, standing up.

He raised his hands before him, weaving his mana into a spell. Elara watched in amazement as a giant tree sprouted from the ground before him and shot up into the sky like a tower.

"This is what we do as a warning," Rylan said as he watched the tree grow high up into the sky. "They'll know to stay low when they see it." Then he turned to Elara and said: "let's get you back to the Academy before you get yourself in trouble."

It seemed to Elara as though Rylan had found himself once again, and his concern for her had overtaken his desire for revenge momentarily.

They set off through the forest, navigating their way as best they could with Rylan seemingly able to home in on the right direction, even if he had been blinded by rage on his journey out. Along the way, they talked about Darien and Mara, and Rylan offered his own theories about what might have happened to them.

Elara knew they were earth mages, but Rylan didn't know who they were and hadn't heard of them before. He could only guess that they wanted to simply live a life of solitude without interference from either the Academy or the soldiers from the city.

The pair were deep in conversation when they finally came across the familiar doorway and stairs that led down to the secret Academy.

Elara smiled, feeling the weight of the past few hours begin to lift from her shoulders. She was safe, and so was Rylan, and she had managed to enact her very first spell.

Chapter 8: Betrayal

As they descended the stairs, Elara couldn't help but feel a sense of relief wash over her. She had been worried sick about Darien and Mara, and now that she was back at the Academy and she knew they had been warned of the potential danger, she could finally relax a bit.

Once the pair reached the bottom, they were greeted by the familiar sight of the underground Academy. Elara looked around, taking in the mud and root walls and flickering torches that illuminated the space.

Rylan led her down the hallway, and they soon arrived at her room. Number one four two.

"I think it's best if you rest here for a bit," he said. 'I'll go speak to the Headmaster and see if he has any information on Darien and Mara… and maybe apologise for being an ass."

Elara nodded gratefully. "Thank you, Rylan," she said. "And you were an ass."

Rylan smiled. "You would have been fine," he said. "But I'm glad we're back. I'll be back soon."

With that, he turned and made his way back down the hallway. Elara closed the door to her room and collapsed onto her bed, feeling drained but relieved to be back at the Academy.

As she lay there, Elara couldn't help but replay the events of the past few hours in her mind. She had come face to face with danger, discovered her own powers, and seen a different side of Rylan. She couldn't help but wonder what else lay ahead for her at the Academy.

Elara picked up the locket, feeling its cool metal against her fingertips.

She focused her attention on the tiny lock and closed her eyes, taking a deep breath to calm her mind.

She reached out with the seed of mana inside her, willing it to grow and expand, feeling the energy flow from her body and into the lock. As she concentrated, the energy began to weave around the pins inside the lock, searching for the correct placement so that she could open it.

Her mana moved with a gentle, fluid motion, like threads of silk being woven together. She could feel the individual pins inside the lock, their position and shape, and the precise pressure needed to move them into the correct position.

Slowly, she manipulated the lock with her mana, guiding the mechanism into place one pin at a time. She could feel the satisfying click of each tumbler as it fell into position, until finally, she felt the lock release and the locket clicked open.

Elara opened her eyes, feeling a rush of excitement and triumph as she gazed upon the contents of the locket.

Inside was a small piece of paper folded many times and as she unfolded it, she found a message there.

As Elara gazed down at the message from inside the locket, her eyes filled with tears. The message was a heartfelt letter from Rylan's father.

"My dearest Rylan," the letter began, "I hope this message finds you well. Your mother and I love you more than words can express, and we want you to know that we are so proud of the young man you have become."

Elara couldn't help but feel the love emanating from the words on the page. She continued reading, her heart heavy with emotion.

"Life is full of ups and downs, my son, and we know that you will face many challenges in the years to come. But always remember that you are strong and capable, and that you have a heart filled with love and kindness. Always do what is right, and make us proud."

As Elara finished reading the letter, she couldn't help but feel a deep sense of sadness. Rylan had lost so much, and yet he still managed to be a caring and strong individual.

She carefully placed the letter back inside the locket and closed it, feeling a sense of gratitude for the opportunity to have read such a personal and touching message.

The next morning, Rylan joined Kaelin, Anya, Landon, and Elara for breakfast in the courtyard after they had all traded pleasantries and brought their food to a large wooden table. As soon as he sat down, they all began to tease him about his disappearance the day before.

"Good morning, sleepyhead," Kaelin said with a grin. "Did you have a nice nap in the forest?"

Anya chimed in, "Yeah, we thought you might have found a comfy spot and decided to spend the night out there."

Landon added, "Maybe he was communing with the trees or something."

Rylan took it all in stride, laughing along with them. "Ha ha, very funny, you guys," he said. "I was just taking care of some business."

Elara handed him the locket under the table, their eyes meeting briefly but saying nothing.

Kaelin noticed the exchange and raised an eyebrow. "What's that, Rylan? A secret love note from your girlfriend?" she teased.

Rylan rolled his eyes. "No, it's nothing…" he said, tucking the locket away in his pocket rather sheepishly. "But thanks for the concern, Kaelin."

As they finished their breakfast, the group was interrupted by the Headmaster himself, who approached them with a serious expression on his face. "Excuse me, everyone," he said, "I need to speak with Elara and Rylan. Please follow me to my office."

Elara and Rylan exchanged a worried glance but quickly followed the Headmaster to his office. They walked through a series of hallways and up a flight of stairs, eventually arriving at a large wooden door with an intricate carving of the growing tree. The Headmaster pushed it open, revealing a spacious office with high ceilings and large windows that let in streams of sunlight. It was strange because Elara was absolutely sure they were still underground.

The room was adorned with elegant furnishings, including a polished oak desk, a plush rug, and a bookcase filled with leather-bound tomes. The walls were lined with paintings and tapestries depicting some kind of battle, and a small table in the corner was set up with tea and pastries.

The Headmaster motioned for them to sit in the two comfortable armchairs in front of his desk before taking his own seat. "I have some troubling news," he began, his voice grave. "I have received word from a trusted source that Darien and Mara have been captured by soldiers from the city and are being held captive." A bird just outside one of the windows flapped its wings as though to punctuate its presence. "I need you to tell me everything that happened to you yesterday and also what you know about this pair."

Elara and Rylan sat in stunned silence, unsure of what to say. The Headmaster continued, "Our source also reports that they are being tortured for information. So we must act quickly so that we know the level of danger we are in."

Elara spoke up. "They're friends of mine," she said. "I met them before in the forest... I was being attacked by some creature and they saved me. Without them I would never have found the Academy."

The Headmaster nodded. "I see. Can you tell me anything about their current situation or why they might have been captured?" He kept a level tone, but Elara could tell that he was becoming anxious.

Elara looked down, unsure of what to say. "I'm not sure," she admitted. "I haven't seen them since, and they told me not to tell people they helped me. But they're good people. They wouldn't have done anything to deserve this."

Master Arin's expression softened. "I believe you, Elara," he said. "But we could be in grave danger, especially if these two know where we are. It pains me to say this, but I cannot risk the safety of our Academy and its students. Our main mission objective is to remain hidden at all costs."

Elara's heart sank. "But we can't just leave them there to suffer," she said. "They helped me, we have to help them."

The Headmaster sighed. "I understand your concern, Elara. But it is not as simple as that. We do not know the full extent of the danger we are in, and if we were to try and rescue them, it could expose our location and put everyone here in grave danger."

Rylan spoke up. "But what about sending someone in secret to at least check on them and see what's going on?"

Master Arin considered this for a moment before nodding. "That may be possible. But it will have to be done with the utmost caution and secrecy. I will discuss this with our most trusted allies and see what can be done. In the meantime, I need you all to keep this information to yourselves. We do not want to arouse suspicion or attract unwanted attention."

Then the Headmaster turned to Rylan, a stern look on his face. "And you, Rylan," he said. "I understand that you left the Academy yesterday to fight the soldiers."

Rylan nodded, feeling slightly embarrassed. "Yes, sir. I just couldn't sit by and do nothing while they were attacking innocent people."

"I understand your impulse to help, Rylan, but you must understand the importance of our secrecy. We must remain hidden at all costs. If we reveal ourselves, we will be putting not only ourselves but also the lives of every single one of our friends in danger. We cannot allow that to happen."

Rylan nodded again, chastened. "I understand, sir. I won't do it again."

Master Arin's expression softened. "I don't blame you for wanting to help, Rylan. It shows a strength of character that is rare. But please remember that anyone is free to leave this Academy at any time. If you choose to stay, you must understand the risks and follow our rules. Can I trust you to do that?"

Rylan nodded firmly. "Yes, sir. I'll follow the rules."

The Headmaster smiled. "Good. Now, we must focus on the situation at hand."

Elara and Rylan exchanged a nervous glance. They were worried about their friends in the Academy and what could happen if they were discovered by the soldiers. As they left the office and worked their way back to the courtyard, they noticed that the other students had a similar look of concern on their faces. It was clear that everyone was on edge.

Breaching the daylight in the courtyard, they saw Anya, Landon and Kaelin all sat where they had been before, evidently awaiting their return. Then Elara saw something that made her blood run cold. High in the sky, beyond the illusion of the courtyard and clearly above the Forbidden Forest, black smoke was billowing into the sky.

Elara's heart sank, and she knew in her gut that it had to be Darien and Mara's house.

"What's that?" a voice came from another table as somebody else had seen the smoke, then within a moment heads began to turn and eventually all of the students were staring out at the smoke rising in the distance.

Master Arin then silently appeared at Elara's side, looking grim. "Elara, Rylan, I need you to come with me," he said. "It seems we have run out of time. We're going to investigate that smoke. But we must do so quickly and quietly. And we cannot take the risk of alerting anyone else in the Academy. It is imperative that we remain hidden."

Elara and Rylan nodded, understanding the seriousness of the situation. Anya, Landon, and Kaelin stood up before the three could slink away, determined to come along as well.

"We aren't letting you go out there alone again, look what happened last time!" Landon said with a confident smile."

Master Arin nodded approvingly at the three students' decision to join them. "Very well," he said. "But you must understand that this is extremely dangerous. We do not know what we are walking into. And if we are discovered, it could mean the end of the Academy."

The now group of six set off out of the Academy and towards the black smoke. They moved quickly and quietly through the trees, and the smoke grew thicker and blacker as they got closer and closer to its source. As they moved they remained silent.

Elara's heart raced with fear for what they were going to discover.

As they approached the edge of a clearing and the clear source of the billowing smoke, they saw the smouldering ruins of a small cabin, barely visible through the thick smoke. Master Arin motioned for the group to stay back as he approached the cabin, his palms held up as though he was ready to defend himself.

Elara and the others watched silently as he entered the cabin, disappearing into the darkness. Minutes ticked by, and Elara could barely stand the suspense. Finally, Master Arin emerged from the cabin and signalled for them to come closer.

Elara's heart sank as she saw the devastation. The cabin was completely destroyed, reduced to smouldering ashes. And there was no sign of Darien or Mara.

Master Arin turned to Elara and the others, his eyes wide with sudden realisation. "This is a trap," he said. "To lure me out here alone… I fear that we are all in great danger…"

The group was stunned, unsure of what to do next. Elara felt a chill run down her spine at the thought of danger lurking in the shadows. She knew that they needed to act fast, but what could they do?

"We need to get back to the Academy," Master Arin said, breaking the silence. "We must warn the others and prepare for an attack. They will be coming for us soon."

As Master Arin finished speaking, the sound of rustling leaves and snapping twigs caught their attention. They turned to see a group of men emerging from the forest, their armour clanking as they advanced towards the group.

Elara's heart raced as she realised the danger they were in. These were not ordinary soldiers, but skilled mercenaries hired by the kingdom to capture the elusive Academy and its Headmaster. She'd seen people dressed like this before.

Master Arin stepped forward, and as he separated his hands, a long, thick wooden staff materialised between them. "What do you want?" he demanded, his voice steady and calm despite the danger.

One of the mercenaries stepped forward, a cruel smile on his face. "We're here for the Headmaster and his Academy," he said, his voice dripping with malice. "And we know you're hiding them here."

Master Arin stood tall, his eyes scanning the group of mercenaries. "I'm sorry to disappoint you," he said, his voice laced with authority. "But there is no Academy here. You're wasting your time."

The mercenaries laughed, clearly not believing him. "That isn't what your friends told us," another one said. "We know you're here in the forest. And we're not leaving until we find what we came for. Either that or we'll burn the entire thing down to the ground."

Elara and the others stood frozen with fear, unsure of what to do next. They knew that Master Arin was their only hope, but the mercenaries seemed determined to capture him and the Academy.

Rylan then stepped forward to stand in line with Master Arin. He reached down to his side where his sword would have been if he'd carried it and magically unsheathed a green blade of wood and vine. It was clearly a sword and despite the material it was constructed from, it looked both sharp and deadly.

Chapter 9: Training 2

Elara and Kaelin looked at each other with fear in their eyes, knowing they were not skilled enough to defend themselves but thankfully, Anya and Landon quickly stepped forward to protect them, each beginning to weave their mana as they stood to the ready.

Anya closed her eyes and focused her mind, willing a thick wooden dome to grow up around the group, protecting them from any incoming attacks. The wooden dome formed quickly and it was clear that Anya could feel the weight of her magic draining her energy.

Landon, on the other hand, focused on the roots of the trees around them. He reached out with his magic and summoned them to his command, causing them to shoot up from the ground and wrap around the legs of the mercenaries. Some of the mercenaries tripped and fell, while others were held down by the roots.

Then Master Arin and Rylan engaged the mercenaries in battle. Master Arin used his wooden staff to deflect incoming attacks expertly, while Rylan moved quickly and gracefully, dodging and striking with his wooden sword. The mercenaries were skilled fighters, but the two mages were clearly able to hold their own.

Elara and Kaelin watched in awe at the magic flowing all around them. They felt safe within the wooden dome created by Anya and watched as Landon's roots held the mercenaries at bay. It was clear that their friends were skilled mages, but they also knew that this was just the beginning of the fight to protect the Academy.

But with sheer numbers, the mercenaries began to overwhelm Rylan.

who was starting to tire. Though it had proven durable, his wooden sword was showing signs of wear and tear, and his movements were becoming slower and less graceful. One of the mercenaries took advantage of Rylan's exhaustion and landed a solid blow, causing him to stumble back, his sword falling from his grasp.

Elara watched in horror as Rylan was overpowered. She couldn't just stand there and watch her friend get hurt. In a moment of desperation, she screamed out, hoping to distract the mercenaries.

Her scream seemed to do more than just that, however. It caused Master Arin to turn and look in her direction. Suddenly, his eyes glowed bright green, and he lifted his wooden staff high into the air.

A powerful surge of magic flowed from Master Arin, and the ground beneath the mercenaries shook violently. The trees swayed back and forth, and the mercenaries were thrown off balance. The wooden dome around Elara and the others crackled with energy, but it held firm.

As the magic surged, a huge wave of green energy burst forth from Master Arin's staff. It washed over the mercenaries, knocking them back and leaving them dazed and disorientated.

Rylan seized the opportunity to recover, and with renewed vigour, he leapt back into position beside the Headmaster.

The pair were about to renew their attack, when the thundering sound of footsteps shook the ground and through the trees came three great beasts and as soon as the three beasts entered into clear view, Elara couldn't help but whimper. She'd seen these things before and cowered in the presence of the Grimscales.

As the Grimscales charged towards the mercenaries, the men scattered in fear, dropping their weapons and fleeing in all directions. The massive creatures, covered in fur and black scales with razor-sharp claws and menacing beaks, roared with fury as they launched themselves at the mercenaries. The ground shook beneath their feet as they barrelled through the forest, ripping apart the trees in their path.

Master Arin, Rylan, Anya, Landon, Elara, and Kaelin seized the opportunity to escape and as soon as the protective wooden cage fell back into the ground, they regrouped and made their move. They ran away from the clearing as fast as they could, the deafening roars of the Grimscales and screams of the soldiers following them as they moved.

Finally, the group reached the Academy, and the students all collapsed onto the ground, panting and gasping for air.

"What were those creatures? I've never seen anything like them before," Anya asked, sweat beading on her forehead.

"They were Grimscales," Elara replied with a shudder. "Massive, terrible creatures. I've met one before actually."

Anya gave her an inquisitive look, but before she could ask any more questions, Master Arin spoke, his expression grave.

"I need to go to the city. I need to know if we are all still safe here," he said, his voice filled with concern. "You'll all have to look out for each other while I'm not here, but you must promise that you won't go out into the forest until I return."

"What should we do while you're gone?" Anya said, her eyes wide with fear.

"You should remain here, inside and safe," the Headmaster replied. Then he added almost as an afterthought: "and perhaps keep training. You never know when those spells of yours are going to come in handy."

After Master Arin had left, the group all made their way to the training sands that Elara and Rylan had practised their swordsmanship on. Elara knew at least a part of what each of the rest of the group could do – save for Kaelin, who she'd yet to see cast a single spell – but she didn't know *how* any of them did what they did.

"Everyone's mana is different," Rylan explained to Elara as she watched Anya pull a protective dome over herself for the tenth time in a row. "There are some standard spells that you can learn that utilise the mana in similar ways, but when you start being able to control your mana properly, that's where the real differences start to show."

Elara nodded, watching as Landon lifted his arms and the ground beneath them began to ripple and shake. Suddenly, thick vines and roots burst from the earth, wrapping around training dummies and pulling them down.

"That's incredible," Elara said, genuinely impressed. "How did you learn to do that?"

Landon grinned. "It's just how my mana works. Remember how I told you my mana is like a rock in a river? My spell works on that principle, holding people down like a rock while my mana is like the water flowing around them."

Anya walked over, her wooden cage now surrounding Rylan. "And how about you, Rylan? How did you learn to fight with a wooden sword? Just started doing it when you were a kid and could never stop?"

Rylan chuckled. "Well, I've always loved the idea of sword fighting, so I make my sword and taught myself how to use it. I've been practicing for years now and this way there's always a sword ready to go."

Elara was fascinated by the diversity of their abilities and how each of them had found unique ways to use their mana. She felt a sense of admiration for her fellow students and their creativity.

"I'm impressed," she said, smiling at all of them. "You all have such incredible abilities. I feel like I still have so much to learn."

Kaelin, who had been quiet until now, spoke up. "We all have something to learn. That's why we're here at the Academy. We're all here to become better than we are now... some more than others," she glanced at Rylan with a smirk. "But remember Elara, these three are Master ranked. They have such great control over their mana, you shouldn't be trying to copy them yet, even if your mana worked like theirs did. You're an Apprentice and I'm a Journeyman, and there's only so much we can do right now."

Elara nodded thoughtfully.

"So what is the difference between an Apprentice and a Journeyman anyway? And how long does it take to increase your rank?"

Kaelin smiled at Elara. "An Apprentice is someone who is just starting out, learning the basics of magic and mana control. A Journeyman has a bit more experience, having learned the basics and honed their skills. As for how long it takes to increase your rank, it really depends on the individual. Some people may take years to become a Journeyman, while others may advance more quickly."

Rylan spoke up. "And becoming a Master takes even more time and dedication. It's not just about being able to control your mana and cast spells, it's also about understanding the deeper principles of magic and how to apply them."

Anya nodded. "That's why we have the Academy, to help us learn and grow as magic users. It's not just about the individual, but also about the community and how we can work together to become stronger."

"But where do I even start?" Elara asked in almost a whine.

"That is exactly why journeymen teach Apprentices and Master teach journeymen," Kaelin said with a smile. "Because we were just like you not so long ago. There are one or two spells that manifest in most mages at Journeyman level, so you have somewhere to start at least."

Kaelin then held both of her hands out in front of her, towards Elara.

"Feel my hands," she said with a smile.

Elara hesitated for a moment, then took a hold of both of Kaelin's hands. She was shocked to note that they felt cold to the touch, and solid as though they were made of wood.

"This is a basic spell that uses your mana to harden your skin. It's helpful for defending yourself and it's one of the first spells all earth mages get taught. I call it 'Harden', but you can call it whatever you like."

Elara was fascinated by the spell Kaelin had just shown her. She had never seen anyone use magic to harden their skin before. She released Kaelin's hands and held out her own, trying to feel the difference between their skin. Kaelin's hands were definitely harder than hers.

"Can I learn it too?" Elara asked with excitement.

"Of course you can," Kaelin replied with a smile. "But first, you need to learn how to control your mana. It's not just about having the ability to use it, it's about controlling it too. And that's where we come in, to guide you and help you learn."

Rylan nodded with a smile. "It takes time and practice, but with dedication, you'll get there."

Anya added, "And remember, everyone's mana is different, so your journey will be unique to you."

Elara felt the surge of determination build within her and held her hands out before her as Kaelin had. She closed her eyes to focus on her mana once more, nurturing her seed and willing it to grow.

"Does she always make that face?" Rylan asked. "Just asking for a friend."

"Your wooden sword is as dull as your wit," Kaelin replied and Elara opened her eyes to see that at least the pair were smiling.

"At least my sword won't give me splinters," Rylan retorted, twirling his weapon expertly. "How many did you get the first time you cast that harden spell of yours?"

Kaelin rolled her eyes. "Your sword is practically a twig, it's a wonder it hasn't snapped in half yet."

Rylan smirked. "I don't need a big sword to defeat my opponents. I have skill and finesse."

"More like luck and clumsiness," Kaelin teased, winking at Elara who was still watching them with amusement.

Rylan pretended to look offended. "How dare you insult my honour! If we weren't helping Elara right now, I'd challenge you to a duel!"

Kaelin laughed. "OK twig-boy. We'll put that on hold, just be prepared to lose."

Elara couldn't help but smile at their playful insults and the camaraderie between them.

Elara took a deep breath and closed her eyes once more, focusing all her attention on her mana. She could feel the seed within her growing stronger and larger, its roots reaching out and intertwining with her own being. As she concentrated, she felt the mana within her body start to flow more easily, like a river that had been unblocked.

She held out her hands once more and focused on how Kaelin's hands had felt in hers. She imagined the hardening magic as a layer of wood solidifying over her skin, protecting her from harm. She tried to channel her mana into the spell, but nothing seemed to happen.

Elara opened her eyes and sighed in frustration. "It's not working," she said, disappointment clear in her voice.

Anya smiled encouragingly. "It's okay, Elara. Just keep trying. It takes time and practice to Master any magic."

Elara nodded and closed her eyes once more. She focused on the seed within her, feeling its energy radiating throughout her body. She imagined it growing, branching out like the roots of a tree, until it enveloped her entirely just like she had done with the locket.

As she focused, Elara could feel a tingling sensation spreading across her skin, as though something were happening. She held her breath, concentrating on the feeling. Suddenly, she felt a jolt of energy, and her skin hardened as though it were made of wood, the mana spread out over her entire body.

Elara gasped in amazement and opened her eyes. She looked down at her hands and saw that they were covered in a layer of rock-hard skin. She could feel the magic coursing through her, and she couldn't help but smile. As she removed her attention from her mana, the layer abated and her skin returned to normal.

"I did it!" she exclaimed, holding out her hands for the others to see but there was nothing notable to see.

Rylan grinned. "See? I told you it just takes practice."

Kaelin nodded, a proud smile on her face. "Well done, Elara. You're a natural."

Anya clapped her hands in excitement. "That's amazing! You're already making progress."

Chapter 10: A Knock in the Dark

As Elara prepared for bed, she couldn't help but think about her progress with the harden spell. She had managed to hold the hardened skin for a few seconds before it dissipated, but she knew that with more practice, she could make it last longer. She climbed into bed, feeling exhausted but also excited about her progress.

As she was about to drift off to sleep, there was a soft knock at her door. She sat up, wondering who it could be at this hour. When she opened the door, she was surprised to see Rylan standing there, looking nervous.

"Is everything okay?" Elara asked, concerned.

Rylan hesitated for a moment before speaking. "I need to talk to you about something. Can I come in?"

Elara nodded, stepping back to let him in. Rylan walked over to her desk and sat down on the chair, and placed the locket she had previously opened on the table.

"What's wrong?" Elara asked, taking a seat on her bed.

"I know I may seem like I always know what I'm doing, and I put up a good front and all... but I just want you to know," then he added quickly: "and it's the same for all of us really, but a lot of the time we just kind of close our eyes and hope. I remember what it was like to be the only one not able to control their mana or to cast spells, but I promise it'll come, and it'll get easier."

Elara felt a surge of warmth in her heart and she smiled. "And you came all the way here, now, to tell me that?"

"Well..." Rylan said slowly, his feet fidgeting. "I wanted to explain about the locket…"

"It's from your father, right?" Elara interrupted. "I read the note inside." Instantly she felt like an idiot. The note had been personal and she hadn't ever really asked if she had been allowed to read it.

"It is… but it's OK," Rylan said. "It's just that I'm pretty good at keeping a guard up around here, I can act a little differently around people so they never really get to see…" he trailed off but Elara knew what he was about to say. It wasn't going to be anything as cheesy as 'the real me', but it wasn't going to be too far off.

"I left my parents behind," Elara said slowly. "I couldn't have them throw everything away just because my eyes were suddenly green."

Rylan nodded in understanding. "We will be the best mages we can be, and we will make our parents proud. Their sacrifices won't be wasted, and I'll do everything I can to help you too, Elara."

Again Elara felt a warmth wash over her and she couldn't help but smile.

"Thank you, Rylan," she said quietly. "I don't know what I would have done if it wasn't for you and the others."

"You would've been fine," Rylan said with a smirk, finding his cocky persona once more. "Besides, you've got the best of the best to guide you now, right?"

"You mean Anya?" Elara said with a cocky smile of her own.

Rylan chuckled. "Well, of course Anya is great, but I was actually referring to myself," he said, giving her a playful wink.

Elara rolled her eyes, but couldn't help but laugh. "I think we're all pretty great in our own ways," she said. "But speaking of Anya, have you seen her wooden cage spell? It's amazing."

Rylan nodded. "Not one for defensive spells myself actually. But I did like Landon's spell earlier today. The one that shoots roots and vines from the ground? Now that's useful."

"Do you think I'll be able to do spells like that?" Elara said in a small voice.

Rylan nodded. "Absolutely. It just takes practice and patience. Remember, even the most talented mages started somewhere. You just need to keep working at it, and eventually you'll get there."

Elara smiled gratefully. "Thanks, Rylan. I appreciate your encouragement."

"Anytime, Elara," Rylan replied, getting up from his chair. "Well, I should probably get going. We have another long day of training tomorrow, and I don't want to be too tired."

Elara nodded, standing up as well. "Goodnight, Rylan."

"Goodnight, Elara," Rylan said with a smile, before turning and leaving her room without another word.

The next morning, Elara and the rest of the group gathered in the courtyard for their training session. They had decided to change locations from the purpose-made training arena simply because it was perpetually warm and sunny outside, a stark contrast to the underground caverns that constituted most of the Academy. It was also now abundantly clear that some illusion spell was keeping the courtyard hidden from the rest of the forest, so they didn't have to worry about being seen by any nosy soldiers.

Regardless of the sun though, there was an air of tension among the group as they waited for Master Arin to return. They were sure that he was OK, being a powerful Archmage, but the fact that he was still away from the Academy gave the students a sense of loss, like the Academy wasn't truly whole without him there.

"I wonder what's taking him so long," Anya said, breaking the silence as each of them sat silently, practising controlling their mana.

"I hope he's alright," Landon added, looking worried.

Just as Elara was about to say something, a hawk swooped down and landed on a nearby tree branch. It was immediately clear that it had a note tied to its leg.

"That's strange," Rylan said, pointing to the hawk. "I wonder where it came from."

Elara approached the bird and carefully untied the note from its leg. The hawk made no moves as though it felt threatened, and just stood there to allow Elara to unfasten the string around its leg. As she unfolded the note, she saw that one side was a poster with the words "Powerful Archmage to be executed in two weeks," written in bold letters and beneath it a picture of Master Arin.

Elara's heart sank as she read the words. She couldn't believe what she was seeing.

"What does it say?" Anya asked, sensing Elara's distress.

Elara handed the poster to her and watched as Anya's face paled.

But then Elara noticed something. There was writing on the back of the poster, and she quickly had Anya turn it over so they could read it. It was a handwritten note from the Headmaster himself.

"Master Arin was ambushed by the soldiers in the city," Anya said for the benefit of the others after she had finished reading, her voice trembling. "They're going to execute him in two weeks' time in some public show."

The group exchanged worried glances, unsure of what to do next.

"What are we going to do?" Landon asked, finally breaking the silence.

"We can't just let them kill him, can we?" Elara said, her voice very small. "We need to do something, right?"

Rylan nodded in agreement. "But what can we do? We don't have the skills or the resources to take on the city guard. And besides, if they can capture and hold an Archmage..."

"Maybe not alone, but we can't just sit here and do nothing," Anya said, her voice determined. "We need to find a way to save the Headmaster and protect the school. We've been pushed around for long enough by Roderick and his oppressive regime!"

Elara peered at Anya, now hearing and seeing another side to the usually kind, caring and placid girl.

The group fell silent, each of them deep in thought. They knew that time was running out, and they needed to devise a plan fast.

"I have an idea," Elara said, breaking the silence. "But we'll need to act quickly and with precision."

The others looked at her with interest, and Elara continued. "We could use our magic and work together to create a distraction in the city. While the guards are busy dealing with that, we can sneak into where he's being held and free Master Arin."

"That's a risky plan," Rylan said immediately, his brow furrowed in concern. "What if we get caught? And besides, we don't even know where he's being held."

"We have to take that risk," Elara said firmly. "We can't just sit by and watch as the Headmaster is executed. We owe him too much. And besides, we can…" She looked around for something to help her finish her statement, when her gaze fell back to the bird still sat on the branch. "We can reply to his message with the hawk! The Headmaster himself can tell us where he's being held!"

The group fell silent once again, contemplating the plan. After a few moments, they all agreed. It seemed like a bit of a long shot, but they had nothing to lose.

"Alright then," Landon said, standing up. "We've got a lot of work to do, and not very much time to do it." He exchanged glances with Anya and Rylan.

Rylan placed a hand on each of Elara and Kaelin's shoulders. "But you two are going to have to get much better and quick. We aren't heading off into that city without the best chance we have. You're about to get trained by the best three Master this Academy has ever known." He smiled cockily, but Elara could see a flash of worry behind his bravado. She was all for getting better with her magic, but she couldn't help but feel that same apprehension.

"Right," Anya said. "Let's not cut things too fine. Say we train for ten days solid, then that gives us a little leeway to free Master Arin from wherever it is."

~

As Kaelin and Elara turned to face the Master , who had all stepped away to line up before them, they felt a mix of excitement and apprehension. They had been training and practising their magic as hard as they could already, but with this new development, they knew they needed to seriously step up their game and the added pressure was either going to make or break them.

And now, they were about to receive some more specific instruction from the three Masters with their full attention on powering up the Journeyman and the Apprentice mage.

"Ready to learn how to properly defend yourselves?" Rylan asked with a smile.

"Absolutely," Kaelin replied, trying to sound confident.

"Good," Rylan said, walking up to them. "Because you're going to need it if you're planning on surviving against those soldiers.

"Umm, remember what happened the last time you went out looking for a fight?" Anya asked from next to Rylan. "Didn't Elara have to save you from a trap, then those Grimscales came and saved the rest of us?"

Rylan shut his eyes with a sigh.

"Can't you just let me have this?"

"Nope," Anya replied.

"We're ready for anything," Elara said, interrupting the back and forth.

Rylan smiled. Inwardly he was thankful for the interruption, and he held out both his hands before him.

"OK, harden," he said, and his skin darkened ever so slightly as Elara and Kaelin watched. They had seen the spell before, but it looked so effortless for Rylan to cast like he didn't have to concentrate at all. Elara already knew she could cast the spell, but she also knew she had to keep her eyes shut and take the time to try to coax her mana into the spell as though it was a petulant child.

Landon stepped forward next to Rylan. "Harden is a basic protection spell that every mage needs to Master," he said, his voice carrying authority. "It's a spell that hardens your skin, making it more resistant to physical attacks. But it's not just about casting the spell; it's about sustaining it for longer periods of time."

"Exactly," Anya chimed in. "The longer you can maintain the spell, the longer you can hold off your enemies and give yourself a chance to escape or counter-attack."

Kaelin and Elara nodded, taking in every word. They knew that mastering the basics was the foundation for any advanced spellcasting.

"Let's see what you can do," Landon said, his eyes on Kaelin. "Show me your Harden spell."

Kaelin took a deep breath, closed her eyes, and focused on her mana. She felt it flowing through her veins like a current of electricity. She imagined it gathering in her palms, ready to be unleashed. With a flick of her wrist, she opened her eyes and the spell was cast.

Elara was once again surprised at the lack of effort the others seemed to need to put into the spell, but Kaelin was a rank above her, and the others two, so she looked to that fact for comfort.

Kaelin's skin turned a shade darker, as if covered in a thin layer of hardened clay. She let Elara feel the protective barrier, and it gave her a tiny boost to her own confidence.

"Not bad," Landon said, nodding approvingly. "But you can do better. Focus on maintaining the spell for longer, and try to extend it to cover your entire body."

Elara stepped forward, eager to show her progress. She repeated Kaelin's actions, though it took about twice as long and she kept her eyes closed the whole time. She was also acutely aware that sweat had immediately started covering her face, which itself was reddening. Her skin hardened, but only for a few seconds before it reverted back to its original state.

"You need to work on your concentration," Rylan said, teasingly. "I think you're too busy daydreaming about handsome Master mages and not enough time focusing on your magic."

Elara rolled her eyes, but a smile played on her lips. She knew Rylan's words were meant to be playful, and she couldn't help but feel grateful for the light-hearted moment.

"Let's try again," Anya said, stepping forward. "Focus on your mana and try to extend it throughout your entire body. Don't worry about holding onto the spell right now, you need to get it to feel natural, that way you won't have to concentrate so much on the change it's making."

Kaelin and Elara nodded and closed their eyes, trying to block out any distractions. They focused solely on their magic, feeling it flow through them and imagining it hardening their skin.

After several minutes of practice, both Kaelin and Elara had managed to extend their spell to cover their entire bodies.

"Great job," Landon said, clapping his hands. "You're making progress. Keep practising, and you'll be able to hold off even the toughest opponents."

"How long can you hold the spell for?" Elara asked Rylan, panting slightly after the exertion of training her mana for just a few minutes.

"You know, I don't think I've ever taken the time to find out," Rylan replied, glancing at Landon and Anya. "Fancy a little test?" he asked.

"Alright, let's have a little competition," Rylan announced with a grin. "Whoever can hold the 'Harden' spell the longest wins."

Anya raised an eyebrow. "You sure you want to do this, Rylan? You know I can hold my own against you."

Rylan chuckled. "I'm not afraid of a little friendly competition."

Landon nodded. "Count me in too."

The three Master stepped forward, facing Kaelin and Elara, who were watching eagerly. None of the three closed their eyes, but they all began their spells and let their mana flow through their bodies, hardening their skin.

Minutes passed, and the three Masters remained still and unmoving, their skin turning darker with the Harden spell. Kaelin and Elara looked on in amazement as the minutes turned into ten, then fifteen, and finally twenty.

"Feeling tired yet?" Rylan asked the other two with a smile, though both of them shook their heads although not voicing a reply.

Another five minutes passed.

Landon was the first to falter, his spell dissipating and his skin returning to its normal state. He breathed out heavily as though he had been holding his breath the entire time and Anya followed soon after, her spell breaking loudly as well. Rylan remained still, his skin still hardened.

"Looks like I'm the winner," Rylan said, grinning.

Anya shrugged. "I wasn't really trying anyways."

Landon coughed and added with a smile: "It was a good competition, though."

Kaelin and Elara clapped, impressed with the Master ' skills. "That was amazing!" Elara exclaimed, though in the end, it had been a little boring. She thought that next time perhaps she and Kaelin should throw stones at their hardened skin to make it interesting.

"We'll have to keep practising," Kaelin said, determined to one day hold the spell for as long as the Master had. "I wonder how long the Headmaster can hold his spell for though," she added.

"Don't worry about that for now," Anya said with a friendly smile. "Just keep practising and you'll keep getting better. Rylan here can only hold his spell for longer because he practises all the time and alone. It's a sad life if you ask me."

The rest of the group couldn't help but laugh at Rylan's expense, who said nothing in reply, though turned a slight shade of red.

The three Masters spent the next hour teaching Kaelin and Elara the proper technique for casting the "Harden" spell and holding onto it. They showed them how to focus their energy and channel it into the protective shield, but then attempted to distract them as they held it. Elara found the whole ordeal annoying, but after a while she started to get the hang of ignoring both the distractions, and the effort of keeping the mana nurtured as it held onto the spell.

"You've got the basics down," Anya said finally, nodding approvingly at Elara. "But you still need to focus on making the spell last longer. You don't want to be caught off-guard in the middle of a battle with a weakened shield."

Kaelin and Elara nodded, taking in the advice. They practised the spell over and over again, each time trying to make it last longer than the last.

"You two are really doing well," Rylan said eventually, with a hint of a smile. "But you're going to need to do better than that if you want to survive out there."

"Hey, we're doing our best!" Kaelin protested, grinning.

"I know, I know," Rylan said, chuckling. "But sometimes your best just isn't good enough."

Elara rolled her eyes. "Thanks for the encouragement."

"And hey, what's your best anyway?" Kaelin asked with a grin. "I forgot, was it hitting people with a stick or falling down pits?"

"Come now that's not entirely fair," Anya said. "If my head was that big, I'd always be falling over too."

Kaelin laughed and the sound made Elara smile. She knew she had been lucky to find such friends in this place, and she was going to do everything she could to keep them safe. Even if she was technically the weakest of the bunch.

As the day drew longer and longer, the group knew that they would need to replenish with a good meal, and a good nights' sleep. There would be plenty more practice to be done in the morning and they needed to recover.

"You've made some good progress today," Rylan said quietly to Elara, taking her aside. "But don't let it go to your head. There's still a long way to go before you're ready for what's out there. I want you to try to remember all of the lessons, good and bad. You either win or you learn, get it?"

Elara nodded. "I will," she said softly. She couldn't help but feel so very grateful for Rylan's words of encouragement and she knew just how lucky she was to have him as a friend.

Chapter 11: Journeyman Ranked

The group had eaten together in the underground hall where they had taken dinner each night and had kept to themselves and mostly quiet. They didn't know just how much the rest of the Academy knew what had happened to Archmage Arin, but they didn't want to cause a panic either.

Elara had been surprised at just how tired she was too. Spending an entire day focussing on her mana and trying to cast a spell over and over had pushed her to the brink of exhaustion, and she found that she could barely keep her eyes open whilst eating. A part of her thought that if she'd chosen the soup, then she could very well be looking at a danger of drowning.

Eventually, each of the mages left the table to return to their respective rooms and get a good night's sleep.

Elara had just got into bed and closed her eyes, when a knock at the door startled her.

"What?" she replied, half groggily, half angrily.

"It's me," Rylan's voice replied, and it caused Elara to immediately sit up.

Elara's heart raced as she heard Rylan's voice outside her door. She quickly got up from her bed and walked over to open it. As soon as she did, Rylan stepped inside and closed the door behind him, causing her to retreat to nearer the bed.

"What is it?" Elara asked, her voice filled with concern.

"I wanted to talk to you," Rylan said, his expression serious. "It's about Master Arin."

Elara nodded, waiting for him to continue.

"I think we should keep what happened with the Headmaster a secret for now," Rylan said, his voice low. "I don't want to risk causing panic among the other mages. And we don't really know who we can trust yet."

Elara bit her lip, considering his words. "You think there are spies in the Academy?"

"I don't," Rylan said slowly, "but I can't be sure, and I think we just have to do this alone. We can't risk anyone else getting hurt or captured. We'll find a way to rescue the Headmaster on our own."

Elara nodded slowly, reluctantly accepting his reasoning. "Okay, but what about the other mages? Shouldn't we at least tell the other Master ranks?"

Rylan shook his head and looked a little sheepish. "Actually… there are only three Master ranks in this Academy - me, Anya, and Landon. The rest are Journeymen, except for you of course, as you're still an Apprentice ranked. It's not really general knowledge but that's just how it is. We keep the numbers a bit of a secret just in case word ever gets out, you know?"

Elara's eyes widened in surprise. She had always assumed that there were more Masters in the Academy, but she trusted Rylan's words. 'I understand," she said, "but seriously only three?" she had thought that perhaps they were a little more common than that.

"We have to do what we can to rescue him," she said firmly, determination in her voice. "If I have to train every hour of every day…"

Rylan nodded. "I agree, but we have to be careful. We still don't really know what we're up against yet, and… well I know I'm not always the most level-headed Master-ranked mage out there, but I'd hate myself if anything bad happened to you Elara."

"I…" Elara stuttered, not exactly sure what to say, but eventually settled on: "I'd hate for anything to happen to you, too."

Rylan stepped closer to her, his hand reaching up to cup her cheek gently. "We'll find a way, Elara," he said softly. "Together, I promise we'll be OK."

Elara felt her cheeks flush at the contact, her heart racing at the intensity of Rylan's touch. She took a step back, breaking the contact. "We should get some rest," she said, trying to keep her voice steady and her breathing as normal as possible. "We have more training tomorrow, and I hope a new spell maybe? "

Rylan nodded, his expression unreadable. "Of course. Goodnight, Elara," he said, his tone betraying nothing.

"Goodnight, Rylan," she replied, watching him leave her room before closing the door behind him. As she slowly got back into bed, her mind raced with thoughts of the Headmaster's capture and the dangerous road ahead. But despite the fear and uncertainty, she couldn't shake the fluttering feeling in her stomach whenever she thought of Rylan.

The next morning, Elara woke up feeling more determined than ever. She got dressed quickly and headed to the training sands, where Rylan, Anya, Landon, and Kaelin were already waiting.

"Good morning, Elara," Rylan said as she approached. "Before we start, now that we are all here, I have an announcement to make." He turned to face the others. "Elara has successfully performed a spell and demonstrated her control over her mana. As such, she has hereby been promoted to the rank of Journeyman."

Elara's eyes widened in surprise and excitement. "Really?" she exclaimed. "I didn't even know that was possible!"

Kaelin smiled at her. "Of course it is. Advancement in the mage ranks is based on your ability to control and manipulate your mana. It's not just about learning new spells, but also mastering the ones you already know and being able to properly control your mana."

Elara beamed with pride, feeling a sense of accomplishment wash over her. She had been working so hard to improve her magic, and now it had paid off.

"Congratulations, Elara," Anya said, patting her on the back and giving her a huge beaming smile. "You've come a long way since you first arrived at the Academy."

"Thank you," Elara said, still bursting with joy. She couldn't wait to see what other spells she could learn and Master as she continued to progress in her training.

"Now, let's get back to training," Rylan said, gesturing towards the sands but not before sending Elara a playful wink. "We have a lot of work to do if we're going to rescue the Headmaster and take down whoever is behind this plot."

"So, now you teach me some all-powerful spell to take down all the King's men?" Elara asked with a crooked smile.

Rylan chuckled, shaking his head. "It's not that simple, Elara. Magic is a tool, but it's how you use it that matters. We need to be strategic and think carefully about our actions."

Elara nodded, understanding the seriousness of the situation. "I know, I know. I just can't help but feel excited about being a Journeyman now."

"That's good," Rylan said with a smile. "It's important to take pride in your accomplishments, but remember, with great power comes great responsibility."

Elara nodded again, her mind already racing with ideas and possibilities. She couldn't wait to see what she was capable of with her new rank.

"Actually, there is something I've been working on that we can all try," Landon interrupted and the whole group turned to look at him.

"You remember my entanglement spell? Well it's kind of like that but a little more… well, offensive."

Elara watched as a hungry expression grew in Rylan's eyes. Earth mages were never particularly well-known for their offensive prowess, and she could tell that Rylan yearned for more offensive spells.

"I was thinking," Landon continued. "Instead of multiple vines used to entangle, I could summon a single, sharp spike from underfoot that would impale the soldiers."

Rylan nodded along happily with wonder in his eyes, though Anya looked a little worried.

"What's wrong Anya?" Kaelin asked as she too picked up on the mood within the master.

"It's just… I've never been taught a spell that was supposed to actually hurt, or even kill someone before. We've always created a protective shell, or slowed our enemies down so we could escape… this just seems like it's on a whole other level…"

Elara could see the concern etched on Anya's face and understood her apprehension. She knew that taking a life, even in self-defence, was not a decision to be taken lightly.

"Anya, I understand how you feel," Elara said softly. "But we have to remember that these soldiers are not just our enemies, but the enemy of every mage in the kingdom. They are being controlled by someone else, someone who wants to harm us and the Academy. If we don't stop them, they will continue to cause harm to innocent people. We must do whatever it takes to protect ourselves and those we love." An image of Elara's parents sat in her previous home flashed into her mind's eye and it steeled her statement.

Anya nodded, her expression softening. "You're right, Elara. We can't let them hurt anyone else."

Rylan stepped forward, his gaze firm. "We will do what we must to protect ourselves and the Academy. And if that means using offensive spells, hurting or even killing people, then so be it."

The group all agreed, and Landon began to demonstrate his spell. Elara watched in amazement as after a moment, a sharp spike of earth erupted from the ground and impaled a target dummy.

"Ha!" Rylan announced as he watched, definitely pleased with the spell and the three Masters fell into conversation about how it had been achieved, how each of them could do it, other details like how many spikes could be summoned, and if the spell could be combined with entanglement for maximum effect. It had looked easy to Elara, but when she thought about how she wielded her own mana, she didn't have the first clue about how she could possibly summon a spike from the ground.

Left out of the conversation momentarily, Kaelin turred to Elara.

"I know it's an awful situation, but we don't have to always kill the soldiers, just when it's really necessary. Plus, congratulations on reaching Journeyman rank!"

Elara smiled at Kaelin, grateful for her words. "Thanks, Kaelin. And I know what you mean. It's just that I've never been in a situation like this before. It's all so new to me."

"I understand," Kaelin said with a reassuring nod. "But you have us here to guide you and help you through it. And remember, your power is a gift, and it's up to you to use it wisely."

Elara smiled, feeling comforted by Kaelin's words.

"Hey," Elara said as she remembered something that Rylan had said last night. "Did you know these three are the only Master ranks in the Academy?"

"Woah woah woah," Rylan called out, having heard Elara's announcement. "What we talk about in private is not to be shared!" He had a wide smile on his face but still his message was clear that this secret was to be kept between the group.

"Private…" Kaelin said slowly. Then seemed to arrive at a decision. "You been having secret meetings? What else did he tell you? And how many times did you kiss?"

Elara instantly turned bright red and pursed her lips tightly. She could see that Rylan was now laughing heartily at her discomfort, but Kaelin continued.

"Relax, Elara, I'm just teasing," Kaelin said with a chuckle. "But seriously, Rylan, what's going on? Why keep the Master ranks a secret?"

Rylan's expression turned serious, his laughter fading away. "It's a safety measure," he said. "We don't want anyone outside the Academy knowing our true capabilities. And besides, the ranking system isn't meant to be a competition or a measure of power. It's just a way to gauge a mage's level of mastery."

Kaelin nodded, understanding the reasoning behind the secrecy. "I see. Well, I promise that I won't tell anyone."

"Good," Rylan said, his smile returning. "Now, let's get back to training. We have a lot of work to do. Now I've been thinking. Let's have Landon teach me how to use the Earth Spike thing, and Anya can teach you both her process for casting the protective dome. After all, if we're to be doing the lion's share of the fighting it only makes sense that you have a safe place to retreat into."

Elara had to admit that it was a very good idea, and having a magical dome to hide within whenever she was threatened sounded like a very good idea to her.

Elara nodded eagerly. "That's a great plan, Rylan. I'm excited to learn more defensive spells from Anya."

Anya smiled at Elara. "I'll make sure to teach you everything I know, Elara. And with the way your Grace works, you'll be able to reinforce the dome even further."

Landon stepped forward, offering his help to Rylan. "I'm happy to teach you the Earth Spike spell, Rylan. It's going to be one of my specialties. But maybe in return, you can let me have a close look at that sword of yours?"

Rylan grinned. "Not bloody likely. Let's get started then."

The group split apart, with Landon and Rylan practising the Earth Spike spell while Anya taught Elara and Kaelin the process she used for casting a protective dome.

"Well, here's how I do it," Anya said as she closed her eyes. "I'll slow it down so you can see what's actually happening.

Within a moment, Elara started to see the effects of the spell being cast. On the ground all around them began to sprout thick shoots, roots and vines that wrapped around one another like tendrils. They grew slowly taller, leaning inwards and within a few moments, they had connected and intertwined into the familiar protective dome Elara had seen before.

Elara couldn't help her mouth opening in amazement. "I don't even know where to start…" she breathed as she took in the majesty of the spell.

Anya smiled. "Well luckily, I do. When I started learning the spell, I was making one pair of tendrils reach over my head like an arch. Once I had that down, it was just a matter of patience to start adding more and more until I could make a full dome. So why don't we start there?"

Elara focused on the seed of mana within her, feeling it stir and pulse with energy. She tried to coax it into growth, imagining tendrils sprouting from her fingertips and burrowing deep into the earth. She felt a surge of power within her as the first two roots began to emerge, twisting and arching over each other like a pair of serpents.

It was difficult and exhausting, and Elara could feel her energy draining rapidly as she maintained the spell. But she was determined to make progress, to learn and grow as a mage. With a deep breath, she summoned all her strength and focused on making the roots stronger, thicker, and more intricate.

Meanwhile, Kaelin was also working on the spell, her concentration fierce and unwavering. She was able to generate a slightly thicker arch than Elara, but it was still a struggle for her. Together, the two girls continued to practice, pushing themselves to the limits of their abilities.

Anya watched on, offering guidance and support when needed. "Well done, girls," she said with a smile. "Remember, it takes time and practice to Master a spell. Don't be discouraged if you can't get it right away. Just keep at it, and you'll get there."

Elara nodded, sweat running down her forehead and into her face. Concentrating on the spell seemed so much harder than the Harden spell had been and deep down inside, she worried that this may have been something that she could never master.

But then she took a moment to reflect on how far she had already come in her magical training. Just a few months ago, she had no idea that she even had the potential to become a mage. Now, she was able to cast complex spells and manipulate the elements around her. She had already surpassed many of her own expectations, and she knew that with dedication and practice, she would continue to improve.

With renewed determination, Elara continued to focus on the spell, feeling the roots becoming stronger and more intricate with each passing moment. She could feel the seed of mana within her responding to her efforts, pulsing with energy and growing stronger.

As she opened her eyes, Elara saw that her roots had grown thicker and more elaborate, intertwining in complex patterns that seemed almost organic. She couldn't help but smile at the sight, feeling a sense of pride in her accomplishment.

Kaelin looked over at Elara's roots and smiled, impressed by her progress. "Wow, Elara, those look amazing!" she exclaimed.

Elara grinned, feeling a sense of satisfaction wash over her. "Thanks, Kaelin. Yours look pretty impressive too."

Anya nodded in approval. "Very good, girls. I can see that you're both making progress. Keep up the good work."

The group continued to practice the spell, refining their techniques and pushing themselves to improve. With each attempt, Elara found that the spell became a little easier, and she was able to maintain it for longer periods of time. She experimented with different patterns and shapes, creating elaborate arches and loops that spiralled into and out of the earth underfoot.

As the sun began to set, Anya called an end to their practice session. "That's enough for today," she said. "You've both done well, and I can see that you're making progress. Remember to rest and take care of yourselves, and we'll continue our training tomorrow."

Elara and Kaelin nodded, feeling exhausted but satisfied with their progress.

Chapter 12: Ouch

Elara and Rylan sat together in the shade of a large tree beside the breakfast courtyard. It still amazed Elara that such a place existed seemingly within the horrors of the Forbidden Forest, but if there was one thing that she had learnt of late, it was to not question the magic that surrounded them all.

The warm sun filtered through the leaves above them and Elara watched as Rylan nonchalantly spun his father's locket between his fingers. It made her remember how he'd used it to help her learn how to control her mana.

"Rylan, I wanted to thank you properly for sharing your father's locket with me. It meant a lot, and really helped me begin to control my mana," she said, looking at him with a shy smile.

Rylan smiled back. "Of course, Elara. I'm glad it helped you. And if you keep going at the pace you are now, you'll be a Master in no time."

Elara didn't know exactly how to respond to that, so they sat in silence for a few moments, enjoying the peace and quiet they seldom had the time to enjoy.

"I want to tell you something, Rylan. Something that not many people know about me," she said hesitantly.

Rylan looked at her with concern in his eyes. "Of course, Elara. You can tell me anything. I'm always here for you."

Elara took a deep breath before speaking.

"Soldiers came to my family's home and demanded money every week. They bled my parents dry until there was nothing left. And then they left us with nothing," she said quickly, her voice barely above a whisper.

Rylan looked at her with sadness in his eyes. "I'm so sorry, Elara. That's terrible."

Elara nodded. "It was a hard time for us. But that's not all. I wanted to tell you how I became aware of my mana."

Rylan looked at her curiously.

"It was through anger," Elara said, her eyes meeting Rylan's. "The soldiers were demanding too much money, and I was so angry that I could feel this power building up inside of me. And then, suddenly, my eyes had changed and something had awoken inside of me. I don't know if it makes a difference, but is mana awoken out of anger just as good as any other?"

Rylan nodded, understanding the intensity of the emotions that could trigger a mage's awakening. "I see. It must have been a shock for you. But mana is mana however it was born. You have such a great talent and the ability to learn quickly. You shouldn't let these thoughts hold you back because I see all the good in you, Elara."

Elara nodded, she could tell that Rylan's words were genuine. "It was a shock. But it's also been a gift. I never knew I had this power, but now that I do, I can use it to protect myself and those around me… I just don't want it to turn into anything terrible."

Rylan looked at her with a sense of understanding. "I worry for the mages in this city, Elara. It's not right that they're forced to hide their abilities, or worse, be executed for using them. But I promise you, if King Roderick ever falls, I will do whatever I can to make sure that mages are welcomed back into the city again."

Elara looked at him with a sense of gratitude. "Thank you, Rylan. That means a lot to me."

Rylan smiled at her. "Of course, Elara. We're in this together. And one day, I promise you'll be able to see your parents again."

Elara's eyes widened at the thought of seeing her parents again. It seemed like such a far-off dream, but hearing Rylan's words gave her a glimmer of hope. "Do you really think so?" she asked, her voice filled with a mix of hope and uncertainty.

Rylan nodded. "I do. You have so much potential, Elara. I have no doubt that you'll be able to accomplish great things, and maybe one day, that will lead you back to your parents."

Elara smiled at him, feeling a sense of determination rising within her. "Thank you, Rylan. I'll do everything I can to make that a reality."

She paused for a moment as she looked into his deep, green eyes. She could see the mana within him yearning to come out and before she knew it, she opened her mouth to speak again.

"Rylan, I… I wanted to tell you something else," she began, her voice soft and hesitant.

Rylan looked at her, his expression warm and encouraging. "What is it, Elara?"

"What are you two doing sneaking over here on your own, having private chats about then, eh?" Landon's booming voice interrupted Elara, and she quickly closed her mouth and turned bright red.

Rylan glared at Landon for interrupting their conversation, but then he turned to Elara and gave her an apologetic smile. "I'm sorry, Elara. It seems like we'll have to continue this conversation another time." he said, standing up from his spot under the tree.

Elara nodded, feeling both disappointed and perhaps a little relieved. She watched as Rylan walked away, his broad shoulders disappearing into the distance.

Landon plopped down next to Elara, grinning at her mischievously. "So, what were you two talking about?"

Elara shook her head, not wanting to share her private conversation with Landon. "It's nothing important," she said, hoping to deflect his curiosity.

Landon raised an eyebrow, clearly not convinced. "Uh-huh, sure. Well, I won't pry. But if you ever want to talk about it, you know where to find me."

Elara smiled at him gratefully, thankful for his support. "Thanks, Landon. That's really kind of you."

Landon nodded, his eyes scanning the beautiful surroundings. "You know, this place is really something, isn't it? The way the sun filters through the leaves, the sound of the birds chirping, and the breeze rustling the trees. It's the perfect place to relax and forget about all our worries, even if just for a little while."

Elara felt a sense of peace wash over her. The forest truly was a magical place, and she felt grateful to be able to experience it with her new friends.

As they sat in comfortable silence, Elara couldn't help but think back to her conversation with Rylan. She wondered if she had made a mistake in not telling him how she felt. But then again, she wasn't even sure what she felt. All she knew was that being around Rylan made her feel safe and supported, and she found herself drawn to him in ways she couldn't explain.

"You know, I see the way you look at him, we all do," Landon said, and Elara felt her face redden even more.

Elara's heart skipped a beat at Landon's words, feeling embarrassed that her feelings towards Rylan were so transparent. She tried to play it off coolly, but her voice trembled slightly as she spoke. "What are you talking about, Landon? I don't know what you mean."

Landon chuckled, seeing right through her attempt at denial. "Come on, Elara. It's written all over your face. You have a thing for Rylan, don't you?"

Elara felt her cheeks flush even more, feeling like she was caught in the act. "I... I don't know what you're talking about," she stuttered, feeling like she was failing miserably at hiding her feelings.

Landon shook his head, grinning knowingly. "You don't have to hide it, Elara. We all see the way you two look at each other. And I have to admit, it's kind of cute."

Elara felt a mixture of embarrassment and relief at Landon's words. Part of her was glad that her feelings towards Rylan were not just her own little secret, but another part of her was mortified at the thought of everyone else knowing.

"Even if it was true, it doesn't make a difference, does it? We have loads to do and bigger things to worry about anyway." Elara said.

"Nope, not even a little bit, Landon said with a wide smile.

"What doesn't make a difference?" Kaelin asked as she too plopped herself down under the tree.

"Just our newest Journeyman mage's huge crush on our good friend Rylan," Landon beamed. "Nothing crazy."

"Oh *that*," Kaelin said with a grin of her own.

"You know too?" Elara asked, mortified.

"Elara, I think there are unidentifiable animals in the forest that know. I mean come on."

Elara covered her face with her hands and shook her head. Peering through her fingers she asked: "Do you think he knows?"

"Actually, he's pretty dense you know," Kaelin said thoughtfully. "It wouldn't surprise me if he had no idea at all."

Elara felt a small glimmer of hope at Kaelin's words, but she didn't want to get her hopes up too high. "I don't know, Kaelin. Rylan can be pretty perceptive when he puts his mind to it. I wouldn't be surprised if he knows."

"Well, either way, you'll never know unless you tell him," Landon chimed in.

Elara sighed, knowing deep down that Landon was right. She couldn't keep her feelings bottled up forever, but the thought of telling Rylan how she felt made her nervous. What if he didn't feel the same way? What if it made things awkward between them?

As if sensing her inner turmoil, Kaelin put a comforting hand on Elara's shoulder. "Whatever happens, just know that we're here for you. And if things do get awkward, we'll make sure it doesn't ruin our friendship."

Elara smiled gratefully at her friends, feeling lucky to have such a supportive group around her. "Thanks, guys. You have no idea how much that means to me."

"But also, we're going to tease you about it like you wouldn't believe," Kaelin said with a smile.

"Elrylan? Rylara?" Landon offered playfully. "Ah, we'll figure it out. Anyway, let's get to the sands, we have loads to go through today. Plus, I think it's time we started making an actual plan to save the Headmaster, you know?"

The three all agreed and made their way to the training arena, where they were surprised to find Rylan and Anya already practising. Rylan was casting Landon's earth spike spell and Anya was defending it by either casting a defensive dome, or by making her skin so hard that the spike simply pushed her harmlessly up into the air. Elara was surprised to see too, that other mages that could only have been Journeyman ranked were all upon the sands just watching the two Masters sparring with wide eyes.

Rylan had been lost in thought, barely paying attention to his sparring with Anya. His mind was preoccupied with thoughts of Elara and her recent behaviour around him. He couldn't help but wonder if maybe, just maybe, she felt the same way he did.

But before he could dwell on those thoughts any longer, Anya interrupted his musings. "Rylan, are you even paying attention? We need to focus on our training if we're going to be ready for anything."

Rylan snapped back to attention and nodded. "Right, sorry about that. Let's get back to it."

~

Meanwhile, Elara and Kaelin had decided to leave Rylan and Anya to their duel, facing off as a pair against Landon. They knew it wouldn't be an easy fight, but they were determined to give it their all and besides, it would be good practice.

Landon smirked as he saw the two girls approaching. "Ready to face the might of my earth magic?" he taunted. "I'm not going to go easy on you though."

Elara and Kaelin shared a quick look before nodding in unison. They knew they had to work together to at least last a few minutes against Landon.

As Landon started to cast his first spell, Elara and Kaelin quickly sprang into action. They each focused their magic on hardening their skin as quickly as they could and then placed the spell to the backs of their minds as they had practised. Then, they began to work together to weave a weak defensive dome of roots around them, hoping to protect themselves from Landon's earth spikes.

Landon's first attack was a series of vines that shot up from the ground to try and grab the two girls, but Elara and Kaelin were prepared, and they used their hardened skin to bat away the vines as they approached.

Then, seeing his opening attack fail, Landon switched tactics and tried to cast an earth spike at them, but Elara and Kaelin quickly dodged out of the way, each rolling to either side of the offensive spell.

The fight continued, with Landon casting these two spells over and over, searching for an opening. Of course, the two girls had no offensive spells of their own to cast, and they both knew they would run out of stamina in no time at all, but they kept to their tactics.

But despite Landon's best efforts, Elara and Kaelin held their own, using their defensive skills to keep themselves safe for much longer than any of them had expected. They seemed able to weave their individual, weaker protective domes together so that they formed a thicket of sorts, which proved very effective against Landon's attacks.

Finally though, their stamina faltered and exhaustion set in. The spike that came from underfoot caught Elara in a glancing blow as she tried to dodge out of the way, throwing her into the air and depositing her onto the sand with a loud thud.

"Elara?" Rylan said loudly as he rushed over and knelt over her with a fair amount of concern in his voice.

Elara groaned, feeling the ache in her body from the impact of the earth spike and the ground when she'd fallen. She opened her eyes to see Rylan hovering over her, concern etched on his face.

"I'm okay," she said, sitting up slowly and rubbing the back of her head. "Just got knocked around a bit."

Rylan helped her up and she leaned against him for support, feeling a surge of warmth in her chest as she did so. She quickly shook the feeling off, not wanting to dwell on her crush in front of her friends.

"Nice work, you two," Landon said, clapping his hands together. "You managed to hold your own against me for much longer than I thought you would."

Elara and Kaelin shared a triumphant smile, feeling proud of their accomplishment. But then Anya spoke up, a serious expression on her face.

"As impressive as that was, we need to remember why we're doing this," she said. "We're not just training for fun. We need to be prepared for the worst-case scenario, which is fighting off the city guards and possibly even the creatures in the Forbidden Forest. And we need to be prepared to do it soon, if we want to save the Headmaster."

Her words hung heavy in the air, a reminder of the dangerous situation they were all in. Elara felt a knot form in her stomach, but she knew that Anya was right. They couldn't afford to let their guard down, not even for a moment.

Rylan put a comforting arm around her, sensing her unease. "We'll get through this, Elara. And if we don't, then I'll make a mighty fine-looking corpse."

"Don't say that!" Elara said with a shudder.

Rylan chuckled softly, squeezing her shoulder gently. "I'm just trying to lighten the mood, Elara. We'll do everything in our power to make sure it doesn't come to that."

Elara smiled weakly, feeling a sense of gratitude towards Rylan for his support. She knew that they were all in this together, and that they had to rely on each other if they wanted to come out on top.

"Let's keep training," she said firmly, trying to push her fears to the back of her mind. "We have a lot of work to do, and not a lot of time to do it in."

The group agreed, and they resumed their training, determined to do whatever it took to save the Headmaster and bring down those responsible for his capture.

Chapter 13: A Disturbance

"Run!" the shout echoed through the hallways of the Academy and reverberated off every surface as though it was coming from all around. Elara had been alone on the training sands with her eyes shut, having remained behind after their session that day to practise controlling her mana, and the shout had caused her eyes to snap open.

A young male mage in a robe whom she didn't recognise then ran past her, not even sparing a moment to look at her still sitting on the ground.

Then Elara heard the loud crashing sound of something huge coming towards her down the hallway. She wanted to turn and run, but something inside of her needed to know what was approaching. Her curiosity had got the better of her.

As the creature burst into the training arena, Elara felt her pulse quicken and her hands turn instantly wet; the last time she had faced one of these beasts alone, it had rendered her unconscious, and the next time she had been with a skilled Master ranked mage, and the Headmaster himself who was an Archmage. Alone, she knew that she would not have much of a chance to evade the beast if it saw her.

But the Grimscale did see her. As it shook the sand from its head, Elara watched as its eyes focussed on the wide-open room, and then on her.

Elara could feel her heart pounding in her chest as she took in the massive creature in front of her. The Grimscale was easily ten feet tall, covered in thick, grey scales that shimmered in the dim light of the training arena. Its eyes shone a deep red and it stood on all-fours like it was some terrible dragon-like reptile.

Elara shuffled one foot no more than an inch and the Grimscale let out a low, guttural growl. She knew she had to do something but had no idea what.

Then the Grimscale pounced, and Elara had but a second to react. She willed her mana to flow through her body, to grow and to harden harder and faster than ever before and the Grimscale crashed into her, throwing her across the sands and into the hard wall no less than twenty feet away. She crashed into the wall with a thud and had her spell had not taken effect, she would have been in a bad way, if not killed instantly. As it was, the spell had taken hold and although a little winded, she was no worse for the wear.

Elara wished that the others would have taught her at least one offensive spell, but she knew that wishing for things was going to do her no good. Instead, she focussed on the only other spell that she knew how to cast.

Willing her mana to grow within her once more, to sprout into a mighty thicket from the ground to cover her in a strong, protective dome, Elara cast her spell and watched with wide eyes as the roots, twigs and branches sprouted from the ground and covered her in a small protective dome, a poor facsimile of one of Anya's, but it was something.

As the shell closed around her, she watched as the Grimscale began a new charge, and heard the loud cracking sound as it barrelled into her spell with a renewed determination. She could only hope that her magic was strong enough to hold off the great beast until someone could arrive to help her.

The Grimscale slammed into Elara's dome again with a deafening thud, causing the ground beneath her feet to shake. But the dome held strong, the branches and twigs intertwining tightly to form an impenetrable shield around her. Elara could feel the strain on her mana as she maintained the spell, but she knew that she couldn't let it falter, not even for a second.

The Grimscale growled and clawed at the dome, trying to find a weak point to exploit. Elara watched with growing fear as its claws scraped against the bark, leaving deep gouges in their wake. But still, the dome held strong.

As the Grimscale continued its relentless attack, Elara knew that she couldn't keep the spell up forever. Her mana was rapidly depleting, and she could feel her strength waning. She needed to find a way to end this, and fast, but she was already so tired.

Then as though in answer to her prayers to end the fight, the Grimscale managed to use its claws to pull the dome clean from the ground to reveal Elara helpless and defenceless beneath. Again she did the only thing she could think of, curling into a ball on the ground and casting her Harden spell as fervently as she could manage.

The final killing blow did not come though, and Elara opened her eyes.

The face of the Grimscale was only a foot from hers and as she stared into its red eyes, she saw something that she hadn't before: an intelligence that betrayed not aggression and hatred, but fear.

The Grimscale was scared. She didn't know why or how it had come into the Academy, but she knew that it wasn't there to hurt anyone.

Elara blinked.

"It's safe here," she said to the beast quietly. "You don't have to worry, or keep fighting. No one is going to try to hurt you."

The beast moved back slightly and Elara took the opportunity to stand up, holding her hands up and open before her placatingly.

As Elara slowly approached the Grimscale, she could see the creature's eyes flicker back and forth, as if it was considering her words. Its breathing had slowed, but it still looked wary and tense.

Elara continued to speak in a soothing tone, hoping to calm the creature down even more. "You're safe here," she repeated. "We won't hurt you. We just want to understand why you're here."

The Grimscale's eyes darted around the room, as if looking for a way out. Elara could see that it was still scared, but there was something else there too - a hint of desperation.

"Elara, are you still here? The creatures in the forest are…" The words came from the other end of the training sands, and Elara saw Rylan enter with a concerned look on his face. When his eyes fell on the Grimscale though, his statement cut off and his face visibly paled.

Elara turned to Rylan and put a hand up to stop him from doing anything rash. "It's okay, Rylan. This Grimscale isn't here to hurt us. It's just scared." She said still keeping her tone soft and unthreatening.

Rylan stood straight and Elara saw that he placed his hands down by his side. She wondered which spell he had planned on casting, but she could ask him later.

"I was coming to tell you," he said slowly. "The creatures in the forest, something's happening. They all seem like they're running from something… I've never seen anything like it before."

Elara's eyes widened at Rylan's words. "What do you mean, running from something? What could possibly scare them all like that?" she asked, her mind racing with possibilities. It was clear that something dangerous was happening in the forest, and they needed to act quickly if they wanted to protect the Academy and its inhabitants.

The Grimscale let out a low growl, its eyes flickering back and forth between Elara and Rylan. Elara could see that the creature was still tense, but it seemed to be calming down slightly in her presence. Plus, it wasn't actually doing anything threatening, so that was a good sign.

"We need to find out what's happening," Elara said firmly, turning back to Rylan. "We can't just sit here and wait for whatever it is to come to us. We need to be proactive." She couldn't help remember that Darien and Mara had said all but the same thing, but forced that thought out of her mind for now.

Rylan nodded. "Agreed. But what about… uh… that," he said, gesturing to the Grimscale who still seemed tense.

Elara thought for a moment before turning back to the creature. "You can stay here," she said softly. "You'll be warm and safe, but you need to promise not to attack anyone or cause any harm."

The Grimscale let out a snort, but she could see its eyes had lost their previous fear and it seemed to be considering Elara's words. Finally, it crumpled to the ground and rested its maw on its front claws, much like a sleeping dog. Elara felt a wave of relief wash over her, and recognised the look of something that was in need of a good few hours' sleep.

"Alright then," she said, turning back to Rylan. "Let's go see what's happening in the forest. But make sure no one comes in here."

Rylan nodded, and the two of them quickly made their way out of the training arena and towards the exit out of the Academy.

As they ran, Elara could feel her heart pounding in her chest, both from the adrenaline of the encounter with the Grimscale and the urgency of the situation. She hadn't had the chance to digest what had happened yet, but she already felt worried by the whole situation.

As they entered the forest, Elara could immediately see that something was very wrong. The normally quiet forest, with no signs of any animals or creatures unless you strayed too far, was deafening.

All around the pair, creatures of all shapes and sizes passed them without a second look.

"What's happening?" Elara had to shout to Rylan over the thundering sounds of thousands of animals passing them.

Rylan simply pointed though and Elara didn't need to be told that the direction he indicated was that of the city. But then she saw it. Between the city and where they stood, from deep within the Forbidden Forest, black smoke was rising into the air again.

Suddenly, Elara felt a strange vibration in the air, as if something powerful or huge was approaching. She turned to Rylan, her eyes wide. "Do you feel that?" she asked.

Rylan nodded. "Yeah, I feel it too. Something big is coming."

As they spoke, the ground beneath their feet began to tremble, and a deep rumbling sound filled the air. Elara and Rylan exchanged a worried look before they heard a deafening roar, and they knew that they were in serious trouble. Whatever was coming towards them was not to be trifled with.

The pair quickly took cover behind a huge tree trunk, watching as a massive creature emerged from the trees. It was easily twenty feet tall, with wings that spanned twice that, and scales that shimmered like diamonds in the sunlight. Its eyes glowed a deep red, and its roar shook the ground beneath them.

Elara felt her heart racing as she watched the creature approach. She had never seen anything like it before, and she knew that they were in serious danger. What was worse was that if the creature continued on its rampage, it would no doubt reach the Academy.

She looked over at Rylan, who had closed his eyes tightly.

"Rylan, what are you doing?" she whispered urgently.

"I'm trying to create a distraction," he replied, not turning to look at her. "Maybe we can lure it away from the Academy."

Elara nodded, understanding the plan. She knew that they couldn't defeat the creature on their own, but if they could make the creature turn back, then at least the Academy would remain safe.

Rylan finished his spell, and a loud crack sounded a few yards away as a huge tree split in two, catching the creature's attention. It turned towards the sound, its eyes narrowing as it searched for the source of the disturbance.

Elara and Rylan took the opportunity to slowly move further away, staying hidden behind trees as they made their way back towards the Academy. But they could still hear the creature's roars and the sounds of its wings flapping as it searched for the cause of the sound.

Then the creature raised its head and let out an ear-piercing roar before it spread its wings fully. The draft that the massive creature caused reached both Rylan and Elara as it began to beat its wings, taking off and up into the sky above the forest. Elara breathed a sigh of relief.

"I think this was a bad idea. We need to get back inside," Elara said quietly. "I think they've mostly passed, but it's time to warn the others. Something's happening out there and if the creatures of the forest are scared of it – especially whatever that monster was - it can't be good news."

Rylan nodded, and the two of them hurried back towards the Academy, keeping an eye out for any signs of danger along the way. As they approached the entrance, they saw that a small crowd had gathered outside, looking worried and scared. Elara recognised some of the other mages, and also Landon, Kaelin and Anya.

"What's happening?" Kaelin asked loudly.

"We don't know for sure, but we saw a massive creature rampaging through the forest," Elara replied quickly. "We managed to distract it, but it could come back at any moment. The rest of the forest too… something's happening out there. It's time we told everyone about the Headmaster and prepare for the worst."

The group looked at each other, and Elara could see the fear and worry in all of their eyes. She knew that they needed to act quickly and decisively if they were going to survive this.

"Everyone, listen up," she said, raising her voice to get their attention. "We need to evacuate the Academy and get as far away from here as possible. Gather your things and meet at the entrance in five minutes. We'll regroup to the east and figure out our next steps from there. It's not safe here anymore."

"No, this is the safest place we've ever known!" one student called back. "I say we go back inside and wait for the Archmage to figure all this out." There were a few nods and a few mumbled words of agreement from the gathered students and Elara knew she needed to tell them about Arin.

"The Headmaster is gone," she said slowly. "Captured by King Roderick's men."

There was a moment of silence before anyone spoke again.

"You're lying!" the same man spoke again. "You come here with a newly awakened mana and now you're telling us all to leave!? Maybe you're just trying to get us all caught. I bet the King's men paid you!"

"Shut up!" Rylan announced loudly.

"Oh and we all know what you want," the man replied. Rylan's face turned slightly red.

Landon, Kaelin and Anya stepped forward to join Rylan and Elara as they faced the other mages of the Academy.

"We're leaving this place, and we think you should all too," Rylan said.

The crowd didn't seem to want to make any move or decision either way, but after a moment the man who'd spoken simply turned and walked away. Following his lead, the rest of the mages all turned and left the group too.

"Oh, and I wouldn't go into the training room if I were you," Rylan called after them.

Chapter 14: Into the Unknown

The group quickly gathered their things and made their way back towards the Academy's entrance. Elara could feel the weight of the situation on her shoulders as she tried to come up with a plan for what to do next. They needed to find a safe place to regroup and figure out their next steps.

"Do any of you have any ideas?" Anya asked.

Elara, Kaelin, Rylan and Landon each had a sombre look upon their faces, but it was clear that nobody had any ideas.

Then Elara had a thought. "If the forest creatures have all run away from nearer the city and have headed east, then can't we move closer to the city and to the west because there won't be anything there?"

Rylan looked thoughtful, then nodded slowly.

"But what about what they're running *from*," Kaelin asked.

Elara sighed. "I don't know, but it's clear that whatever it is, it's dangerous. We need to be careful, but we can't just sit here and wait for it to come to us."

"Maybe we can set up a camp or something, hide it with our spells and see what's going on?" Anya said. "Once we find out what's happening, then we can decide what to do about it."

The group began to make their way west, pressing their way through the trees and underbrush. It was strange, but with her mana properly awakened, Elara felt a kind of kinship with the forest, like it was easier to walk through.

Rylan took the lead having conjured his wooden sword, though it was clear that he was just leading the group in a general direction and not anywhere specific. It was a strange sensation being inside the forest with no sounds around them at all, and it gave Elara a bad feeling.

After about an hour, the group found a small clearing with a stream running nearby and plenty of cover from the thick surrounding trees.

"This looks good," Landon said, scanning the area. "We can set up a perimeter and we'll know if anyone approaches. I'll scout the area to make sure there are no surprises waiting for us."

While Landon went off, the rest of the group began to set up their camp. Rylan and Anya began to set up dense thickets around the perimeter, while Kaelin and Elara worked on teasing existing branches and roots on the ground into two small domes that they would be able to rest in. Within another hour, they had a small camp set up, though they dared not light a fire in case it would lead to their discovery. Thankfully the weather was pleasant and the atmosphere around them all warm.

As they sat around the centre of the camp, eating a meagre dinner of dried fruit and vegetables that Anya had been clever enough to bring along, they discussed their next steps.

"We need to find out what's going on in the city," Elara said, staring at the ground. "We can't just sit here and wait for things to get worse."

"But how do we do that?" Rylan asked. "The city is heavily guarded, and we don't even know what's happening in the forest yet. I don't get what spooked all those animals, but I don't think we're just going to be able to ignore it."

"What if we split up?" Elara said slowly. "Two of us can sneak through the forest and try to get into the city, and the other three can figure out what's going on out here. Then we'll have more information on how we can make a plan to save the Headmaster, and also we'll know if we need to do anything about what's happening out here. If there's a threat to the Academy, then what good will saving Master Arin do anyway? I'll go to the city…"

"No you won't," Rylan replied instantly. "You'd be caught in a second. "Besides, it needs to be two of the Master ranks. I'm going to let you in on a bit of a secret here…" he looked to Anya and Landon before he spoke, who both nodded. "Well… once you can control your mana a little better…" he stared into Elara's eyes as he spoke, and just like that, his bright green eyes faded into a dim brown. A few seconds passed and then the green glow returned.

Elara's mouth hung open.

"It doesn't last long, but maybe enough to fool the guards at the gate," Rylan said quickly. But they'll never know two Masters are truly mages when they tell us to 'open your eyes', and we can go and gather some information.

"I'll go with Anya," Landon said. "You stay here with these two and make sure they don't get eaten." He smiled as he spoke, and in truth, Elara was pleased that she might not be separated from Rylan.

She looked over at Anya, who seemed to be deep in thought. "What do you think, Anya?" she asked.

Anya looked up at her, her expression serious. "I think we need to be very careful. The city is dangerous, and if we're caught, we'll be executed for sure. But if we're careful and stay hidden, we might be able to gather some important information."

Elara tried to remain hopeful. "We'll all be careful," she said. "And we'll meet back here as soon as we can. Hopefully, we'll have some good news. Besides, nothing will happen to us with Rylan fending off all the soldiers with his wooden stick."

Rylan rolled his eyes but couldn't help but smile. "You know it," he said, holding up his wooden sword with a grin.

The group spent the rest of the evening discussing their plans, going over every detail and making sure they were prepared for anything.

Eventually, the dusk began to roll in and they all resigned to the fact that they weren't going to be able to do anything until the morning and first light. The group decided that the best thing would be to get a good nights' sleep so that they would be fresh for the new challenges that tomorrow would bring.

"So I was thinking…" Rylan said with a grin. "Elara and me in this dome, and you three in the other one? Best to keep close together for warmth, no?"

Elara didn't really hear what Rylan had said, but when she looked at the rest of the group, she could see a fair few raised eyebrows.

"You seriously think I'm letting that happen, do you stick boy?" Kaelin said. "I'll be joining you for the night, don't you worry."

Rylan chuckled. "Well, the more the merrier," he said, his eyes twinkling mischievously. "But seriously, let's get some rest. We'll need all our strength tomorrow." The group settled into their makeshift beds, and Elara found herself feeling grateful for the warmth of Kaelin next to her. Her friend slept on her left, while Rylan slept on her right. Each time he breathed in, his chest expanded and brushed against her. She had no idea how she was going to get any sleep.

Elara tried to relax and focus on her breathing, but it was difficult with Rylan's presence so close to her. She could feel his warmth and it was both comforting and unsettling at the same time. After what felt like hours, she finally managed to drift off into a fitful sleep.

When she woke up, the first thing she noticed was the coldness of the air. She sat up, rubbing her eyes and trying to shake off the grogginess. The rest of the group was already up and moving around, preparing for the day ahead.

As she crawled out of the dome, Elara realised that it was much colder than she had anticipated. The ground was frosty, and her breath came out in visible puffs of steam. She pulled her robe around her and joined the others who seemed as though they were ready to go, Anya and Landon wearing nondescript clothes that wouldn't be out of place in the city.

"Good morning," Landon greeted her with a smile. "We're just finishing up breakfast. You hungry?"

Elara nodded gratefully and accepted the bowl of porridge that Landon handed her. She ate in silence, lost in thought about the upcoming day. She was nervous about the others sneaking into the city, but at the same time, she was worried for what her, Kaelin and Rylan might find happening in the forest.

"Be safe," Elara said, hugging both Anya and Landon. "We'll be waiting for you here."

"We'll be back as soon as we can," Landon said with a smile, before he and Anya disappeared into the forest.

The remaining group watched them go, feeling a mix of nervousness and excitement. They knew that the coming days would be difficult, but they were determined to do whatever it took to save the Headmaster and protect the Academy.

"So, ready for a little sleuthing?" Rylan asked with a smile, to which both Elara and Kaelin shrugged in confusion.

"Sleuthing," Rylan repeated, chuckling. "You know, investigating, gathering information. It's what we're going to be doing today."

Elara smiled, feeling a little silly for not understanding the term. "Of course," she said. "Let's get started then."

The three of them set off into the forest, heading in the opposite direction to where Anya and Landon had gone. Elara could feel the tension in the air, and she could see that Rylan and Kaelin were feeling it too. They moved quietly and cautiously, aware that they were heading towards the unknown and possibly grave danger.

As they walked, Elara again couldn't help but think about how strange it was that the forest had gone so quiet. It was usually so teeming with life and sounds, but still it was eerily silent. She wondered what could have caused such a sudden change. Whatever it was, she was sure that it was going to be frightening.

After a while, they came across a clearing that had clearly been used recently. There were footprints in the mud, and the remnants of a campfire. Elara looked around, feeling uneasy.

"This is definitely not natural," Kaelin said, her eyes scanning the area. "We need to be careful."

Rylan nodded. "Let's split up and look around. We might find something that will give us a clue about what's happening here."

Elara and Kaelin headed off in one direction, while Rylan went in the other. As she walked, Elara couldn't shake the feeling that they were being watched. She scanned the trees, but couldn't see anything out of the ordinary.

Suddenly, she heard a twig snap behind her. She spun around, her stomach lurching but there was nothing there. She could feel her heart pounding in her chest as she searched for the source of the noise.

"Elara?" Kaelin's voice came from behind her, and she jumped in surprise.

"Sorry, I thought I heard something," Elara said, trying to calm her racing heart.

Kaelin nodded, looking around cautiously. "Let's keep moving. We don't want to be caught off guard. Maybe we should go back to Rylan."

Elara nodded, relieved to have Kaelin with her. They made their way back to where Rylan was waiting and told him about their findings.

"Definitely something strange going on," Rylan said, his brow furrowed in thought. "We need to keep investigating."

The three of them continued to search the area, moving slowly and carefully. They found more evidence of recent activity, including broken branches and footprints that didn't belong to any animal they knew of. It was clear that someone, or something, had been through this area recently.

As they walked, Elara still couldn't shake the feeling that they were being watched. She kept turning around, expecting to see something, but there was nothing there and she felt her nerves beginning to fray.

"Elara, are you okay?" Rylan asked, noticing her unease.

"I feel like we're being followed," she admitted, her voice barely above a whisper.

Kaelin and Rylan exchanged a glance. "Let's pick up the pace," Rylan said, his voice low. "There's definitely something strange around here and it feels like we're getting closer."

As the group continued, eventually the sound of voices reached them from ahead, and slowing to a creep, they tucked themselves in behind a thick tree. Ahead, they could see a camp full of soldiers from the city.

Elara immediately felt her anger growing inside her, then realised what had happened the last time Rylan had come across soldiers and turned to comfort him. When she saw his face though, he didn't look angry, more curious if anything.

"What are they doing here?" Kaelin whispered, her eyes scanning the camp.

"I don't know, but we need to stay hidden," Rylan replied, his gaze fixed on the soldiers. "We don't want to get caught."

The group watched as the soldiers moved around the camp, some of them gathering around a fire while others patrolled the perimeter. Elara couldn't help but feel a sense of unease as she watched them, wondering what they were doing so far from the city.

"We need to find out what they're up to," Kaelin said, her voice low. "Maybe we can get closer without being seen."

Rylan nodded. "Be careful," he said, his eyes fixed on Elara. "Stay hidden and don't take any unnecessary risks."

Elara nodded, feeling a rush of adrenaline as she prepared to move closer to the camp. She followed Kaelin's lead, moving stealthily and staying low to the ground. They managed to get close enough to overhear snippets of conversation, but could only make out small sections of what was being said.

"Did you see them run? Can't believe the King's finally got something good to use against those creatures," one soldier said.

Elara's heart sank at the soldier's words. It sounded like they were hunting down creatures, likely referring to the magical beings that inhabited the forest. She exchanged a worried glance with Kaelin before they both turned to look at Rylan.

"We need to warn the others," Elara said, her voice shaking with worry. "The soldiers are hunting the creatures in the forest."

Rylan's face darkened with anger. "We need to do something," he said firmly. "We can't just let them continue to harm innocent beings."

"But what can we do?" Kaelin asked.

Rylan thought for a moment before speaking. "But we still don't know what it is they have. Sounds like a new weapon or something."

Elara's mind raced as she tried to think of a plan. "Maybe we could sneak into the camp and try to find out what they're using," she suggested tentatively.

Rylan shook his head. "It's too risky," he said. "We need to find another way."

Kaelin spoke up. "What if we just wait and see what they do next. I know it'll be boring, but then at least we'll know."

"That's a good idea," Rylan said. "But let's move back to a safer distance. We'll be able to see what's happening from further back anyway.

The group kept their eyes on the camp as they crept backwards and eventually, they raised themselves to their feet.

Elara was the first to turn away from the camp, and when she did so she found herself face to face with a huge Grimscale, its eyes burning a deep red.

Chapter 15: Into the City

Anya and Landon approached the city gates, trying to keep their cool as they prepared to enter the city. They had dressed in plain clothes and tried to blend in with the crowds that came and went through the gates as much as possible, but they knew that they would have to be careful if they were going to make it through undetected. If they didn't manage it, they were both acutely aware that the result could very much have been their deaths.

As they approached the gates, two guards dutifully stepped forward to block their way. "Halt!" one of them called out. "State your business in the city."

Anya and Landon exchanged a quick glance before Landon stepped forward. "We're just here to visit some family," he said, keeping his voice steady. "We've been on the road for a while, from the villages to the south of here."

The guard narrowed his eyes, looking them up and down. "Open your eyes," he commanded.

Anya and Landon exchanged another glance before suppressing their mana momentarily, so their eyes wouldn't betray their true identities. They both opened their eyes and looked directly at the guards to reveal normal, brown irises, and the guards seemed to relax a little.

"Alright, you may enter," one guard said, stepping aside to let them pass. "Don't you go causing any trouble in there though, you hear me?"

Anya and Landon breathed a sigh of relief as they made their way into the city. They knew that they had to be careful, and they began to look for any signs of where the Headmaster might be held.

As they walked through the busy streets, they couldn't help but feel overwhelmed by the sheer size of the place. It had been so long since they had walked within, and they had to be careful not to get lost in the crowds.

After a while, they came across a group of soldiers, and Landon could feel his heart pounding in his chest. He knew that they had to be careful, and again they tried to blend in with the crowd as much as possible.

Anya and Landon kept their heads down, hoping to avoid any unwanted attention from the soldiers. As they walked past them, Landon couldn't help but overhear part of their conversation.

"Have you heard about the new prisoners they brought in yesterday?" one of the soldiers asked.

Landon's ears perked up at the mention of prisoners. "What kind of prisoners?" another man asked.

The first soldier shrugged. "I don't know, but the rumour is that it's another load of those mages. They've been taken to the stronghold."

Anya and Landon exchanged a glance. The stronghold sounded like it was sure to be the most heavily guarded building in the city, and it was unlikely that they would be able to get in there undetected. But still they needed to be sure that's where the Headmaster was being held.

The two of them continued to wander through the city, keeping their eyes and ears open for any more information that could help them in their mission. Eventually, they came across a tavern that seemed to be popular with the locals and decided to go inside and listen for any rumours or gossip. Both Landon and Anya pulled dark hoods over their heads so that their eyes were hidden. They did look a little untoward, but it was better than the alternative.

They walked into the tavern after someone left so that they could slip in mostly undetected and quickly found a seat without making any moves to go towards the bar.

As they sat at a table in the corner, they could again overhear snippets of conversation about the prisoners that had been brought in, but nothing that was useful to their mission. They were just about to give up and leave when a group of soldiers entered the tavern, their armour clanking loudly.

Anya and Landon froze, hoping that they wouldn't be recognised. They bowed their heads, staring straight down at the table, but then they heard the order for someone to 'open your eyes'. Thankfully it wasn't directed at them.

"Is everything alright?" one of the soldiers asked, looking down at Anya and Landon.

The pair kept their heads down, trying to appear inconspicuous.

"Everything's fine," Landon replied, his voice low.

The soldier paused for a moment, then seemed to accept their answer and turned to leave. Anya breathed a sigh of relief, glad that they hadn't been discovered.

As the soldiers moved towards the bar, Anya listened to their conversation intently.

"I heard that they're going to transfer him to the palace for the execution tomorrow…"

Anya and Landon exchanged a look. They had finally found what they were looking for. And if the Headmaster was going to be transferred, it could be the perfect opportunity to mount a rescue. They just needed to gather a few more details and then get back out into the forest to find Elara, Kaelin and Rylan. They hoped that their friends would have some information about what was happening out in the forest, too.

They listened to the soldiers' conversation a while longer, hoping to gather any more information they could use. But it seemed that the soldiers were only discussing their plans for the night and nothing more. Anya and Landon decided that it was best to leave before they drew any more attention to themselves so they slipped out of the tavern unnoticed and began making their way back towards the city gates.

"So what do we do?" Anya asked. "We can't break into the stronghold and we can't break into the palace… maybe we can attack them while they transfer him?"

"Attack well trained, armed soldiers?" Landon asked with a sarcastic expression. "Plus, Elara and Kaelin can't even pull their mana away from their eyes yet, so getting them through the gate is going to be tricky as it is.

Anya remained silent as she thought. There had to be something they could do, she knew the idea wasn't too far away, but it seemed just out of reach.

Landon could see the frustration building on Anya's face and knew that they needed to come up with a plan soon. "Maybe we could try to create a distraction," he suggested. "If we can draw some of the soldiers away from the Headmaster's transfer, it could give us a chance to make a move."

Anya nodded thoughtfully. "That could work. But what kind of distraction?"

Landon rubbed his chin, thinking. "Maybe we could create some kind of commotion in another part of the city. It could draw some of the soldiers away and give us an opening to get to the Headmaster."

Anya smiled, feeling more hopeful. "I like that idea. But how do we create a commotion? And still, how are we going to get the others into the city?"

Landon thought for a moment before replying. "Maybe we can set something on fire or create a false alarm. As for getting the others into the city, maybe we can create some kind of distraction at the gates. It could draw the guards' attention away and allow them to slip through unnoticed."

Anya nodded, considering his suggestions. "Okay, so what I'm hearing is that your answer to everything is to create a distraction. You know, I'm starting to think you're more muscle than brains."

Landon chuckled. "Hey, distractions can be pretty effective. But in all seriousness, we need to be careful with what we do. We don't want to cause too much chaos or harm innocent people in the process."

"But also, we actually need a plan," Anya said. "Maybe we'll wait and see what the others think. All we know right now is that tomorrow he's being transferred to the palace, so we'll get back to the camp and talk to Rylan, Kaelin and Elara."

"Well that is if Rylan and Elara aren't too distracted," Landon said with a smile.

Anya rolled her eyes. "I'm sure they'll be fine," she said, a hint of teasing in her voice. "But let's not waste any more time here. We need to get back to the others and start coming up with a plan."

Landon nodded, and they began to make their way back to the forest, keeping their heads down and their hoods pulled up to avoid drawing any unwanted attention.

As it turned out, leaving the city was much easier than getting in. None of the guards seemed to care if the people leaving were mages or not, but still they accosted most of the people entering the city. It would be bad news for Elara and Kaelin, but at least they had their distraction plan to sneak them in with.

"Do you think Rylan and Elara will ever get together," Landon asked as they entered into the forest.

Anya chuckled. "I don't know, they do seem to have a bit of a spark between them. But they're both so focused on the mission right now, I don't think romance is really a priority."

Landon nodded, thoughtful. "Yeah, I get what you mean. But it's good to have something to look forward to, you know? Something to fight for."

Anya smiled at him. "I think we all have something to fight for. And we'll do whatever it takes to protect those we love."

The two of them continued to walk through the forest, lost in thought, until they reached the area they had slept the night before.

What they saw before them though, neither had been expecting. Elara,

Rylan and Kaelin were all stood there to greet them each with huge smiles upon their faces, and behind them was a huge creature with dark grey scales, interspersed with feathers, and deep red eyes. Standing at least four metres long on all four legs, was a terrible Grimscale.

"Before you start, let me explain," Elara said as she watched the blood drain from her friends' faces.

"What is it with you and unruly beasts?" Anya said quickly, jerking her head suggestively towards Rylan.

"Hey, just because you could never tame me," Rylan said with a cocky smile.

Elara felt like she wanted the ground beneath her to swallow her up, though a distant thought reminded her that as an earth mage, that was very much something that could possibly happen if she wished for it a little too hard.

"Anyway," Elara finally said to return the group to their true purpose. "It seems like the soldiers have found a way to push the mana away from certain areas of the forest, and the creatures are going insane. Grey here's the Grimscale that broke into the Academy the other day. I think he wants to help us."

"Grey? You gave that thing a name?" Landon couldn't believe his ears.

Grey raised himself to his full height at Landon's words and took a single step toward him.

"Woah woah woah," Rylan said, holding his hands up towards the Grimscale. "These are our friends. They may seem like they'd make a great meal, but trust me, this one's a bit thin," he gestured to Anya as he spoke, "And this one'll give you indigestion."

Grey then sat back down and looked disinterested in the pair of newcomers.

"What makes you think this thing can help us?" Landon asked and in return, the Grimscale snorted loudly.

"Well really it's because of how it already helped us, I guess," Elara said thoughtfully. "Anyway, another pair of hands… uh, claws, can't hurt, can it?"

"Okay, fine. But we need to be careful. We don't know what kind of tricks this thing might be playing."

Elara smiled at Landon. "Don't worry, we'll keep a close eye on him. But first, tell us what happened in the city."

Landon and Anya took turns recounting their trip into the city, and what they had learned and once they had finished their story, everyone fell silent as they tried to figure out how best they could proceed.

Chapter 16: Good Boy

A few hours prior.

Elara had once again found herself face to face with a terrible Grimscale. Her entire being froze as she stared at the gigantic beast that towered over the group of three, and again she found herself unsure of what to do. The creature was massive, easily four times Elara's size, and she could feel the heat emanating from its eyes. Kaelin and Rylan turned around to see what had caught Elara's attention, and when they saw the Grimscale, they both froze as well.

For a moment, there was silence as the two groups sized each other up. Elara couldn't help but feel a sense of fear as she stood before the creature, but she also sensed something else. A kind of intelligence and awareness, and the feeling of recognition. It was almost like the Grimscale was studying them, considering their presence in the forest and trying to decide if they were a threat or not.

After a moment, Elara felt her fear begin to melt slowly away and her body began responding as normal again. Raising her hands towards the Grimscale who still had not moved, she quietly spoke. "It's OK, we aren't here to hurt you," she soothed. Her hands were getting closer and closer to the beast, then, without warning, the Grimscale turned and began to walk away, disappearing into the dense underbrush.

The group stood there in stunned silence for a moment, unsure of what to make of what had just happened. Finally, Rylan spoke up. "That was... unexpected."

"I've never seen anything like it. It's like it was trying to tell you something," Kaelin said.

Elara couldn't shake the feeling that the Grimscale had been trying to communicate with them, but she couldn't quite put her finger on what it was trying to say. She suspected that it was the same Grimscale that had broken into the Academy, but she had no evidence of that fact, other than the fact it hadn't killed them all there and then.

"We need to find out what the soldiers are doing, everything's just not acting right," Elara said.

"The soldiers must have something powerful to affect the creatures like that… but they couldn't be using magic, could they? The King would never allow it," Rylan said thoughtfully.

The group took to the hidden position to watch the campsite and for the longest time, the soldiers did nothing out of the ordinary. The soldiers continued their patrols, gathered around the fire, and some even went to sleep in their tents. It was as if they were just a normal group of soldiers camping in the forest.

It was then that Elara noticed someone within the camp she hadn't seen before. It was a man wearing a well pressed, almost royal, white blazer with gold buttons down the front. His head was entirely absent hair and when any of the soldiers came near to him, they gave him a wide berth. It was clear that whoever this was, he was certainly an important figure.

The group continued to watch the soldiers, trying to gather as much information as they could about whoever this was, when suddenly, they heard a loud noise from the other side of the camp. It was clear within a moment what had caused the sound: the Grimscale had begun its attack.

The creature barrelled into the camp, knocking soldiers flying in all directions. It made a beeline for one of the tents and it looked as though nothing would stop it from reaching it, when the bald man stepped forwards and behind the creature. Elara wanted to shout a warning to the Grimscale, but she knew she couldn't risk capture by the soldiers.

The Grimscale tore into the tent with its sharp claws and Elara gasped as she saw what was now inside, sat quietly in a small iron cage.

The juvenile Grimscale was only the size of a large dog, it's feathers and scales weren't as deep grey as the larger Grimscale's were, and its eyes although huge, were not a deep angry red; they were a bright and friendly orange.

"It must be its baby," Kaelin whispered. "That's terrible!"

Elara turned to Rylan but she could see that his gaze was unfaltering. It looked as though the scene that was playing out before them was a little too close to home for him.

Then the bald man crossed his arms and closed his eyes, and what happened next was something that Elara would never forget. A pulse of energy emanated from the man that spread quickly towards the group, passing through each of them in a moment and then they felt it; the mana that resided within them all had flickered out of existence.

The Grimscale too, found that whatever the man had done, had affected it in a big way. Elara watched as the creature reared up into the air as though it was battling some unseen restraints, then fell to the ground.

Elara gasped, thinking that the beast had somehow been killed, but she could see its body rising and falling as the soldiers moved quickly to tie the Grimscale up.

"My mana," Rylan said slowly. "It's… gone." He was looking down at his open hands as though in disbelief, and just as Elara was about to try to say something comforting, she saw the green glow flash back into his eyes, and she too could feel her mana return, as though it was the ebb and flow of an ocean.

Relief washed over Elara as she felt her mana return, but the shock of what had just happened left her feeling numb. "What did he do?" she asked, turning to the others.

"I don't know," Kaelin replied, her voice trembling. "But whatever it was, it was powerful enough to affect all of us and the Grimscale."

"We need to find out more about that man," Rylan said, his eyes narrowed in determination. "And we need to free that Grimscale."

Elara nodded thoughtfully. "Do you think he can do that again, and to us?"

Rylan placed a reassuring hand on her shoulder. "We'll be careful. And maybe we've just stumbled on how the city is keeping an Archmage like Headmaster Arin locked up…"

Elara nodded, still feeling uneasy. "But how can we free the Grimscales?" She asked.

Rylan looked at Elara and Kaelin with determination. "We need to act now. I can create a diversion while you two sneak in and free the Grimscale and its baby. They haven't tied it up yet, so if we're fast then we have a good chance of getting it free. But if you get into trouble, I want you to run back to the campsite. Don't look back. Don't wait for me, just run."

Elara nodded, feeling a sense of urgency. "Okay, but that man out there… there's something not right about him."

Rylan nodded. "Try not to worry too much, sometimes it's best not to overthink things and just act on pure gut and confidence," he said with a smile. "Elara, you stay close to Kaelin and you two keep an eye out for any soldiers. I'll create a distraction on the other side of the camp and when the time's right, get in there and free those creatures."

Without wasting any more time, Rylan left the girls and made his way around to the far side of the camp. As she watched him go, Elara couldn't help but feel a deep sense of worry for Rylan and she wondered if they were being stupid trying to free these creatures. But deep down, she knew it was the right thing to do.

The pair waited behind their large tree for any sign of the distraction that Rylan had promised to cause and after a short while, Elara began to worry that he may have been caught.

But just as she was about to voice her concerns to Kaelin, they heard a loud crash and the sound of soldiers shouting in alarm. Elara peeked out from her hiding place and saw another huge tree that had sprouted in the centre of the campsite. The fire that the soldiers had been tending to had been the epicentre of the tree and it caused burning wood, ash and coals to fly in all directions around the camp.

Soldiers scattered immediately and each of them became instantly focused on trying to put out the fires that had started in the chaos. Somehow though, Rylan had managed to angle his spell somewhat, so that the fires that spread were on the far side of the camp, and away from the two Grimscales. And for a moment, Elara could see that they had been left unguarded.

"Let's go," Elara said to Kaelin, and they quickly made their way towards the Grimscale and its baby.

Through either divine intervention, or divine luck, Elara and Kaelin made it to the Grimscales without any of the soldiers even noticing their approach.

There was no time to decide which of the two beasts they should try to free first, though the baby's cage was not locked, only bolted so Kaelin quickly shifted the bolt across and the baby stepped out into freedom. It made it clear though, that it would not budge without its father and Elara quickly moved in to untie him.

The creature looked up at her with its large, red eyes and let out a low rumble. Elara couldn't help but feel a sense of awe at the sight of the majestic creature up close once again, though each time she had been so close, the feeling of danger and fear had lessened.

With the Grimscale freed, Elara and Kaelin quickly made their way back towards the tree line, trying to stay hidden from any soldiers that could have noticed their presence. As they moved, Elara couldn't help but feel a sense of relief and satisfaction. They had managed to free both the Grimscales and now they could hopefully find a way to get them away from this place and deep into the forest and to safety.

But as they reached the safety of the trees, a shout from behind them made them turn around. It was Rylan, running towards them with soldiers hot on his heels.

"We have to go, now!" Rylan yelled, his voice urgent. "They know we're here and they're after us!"

Elara and Kaelin didn't need any more prompting. They took off running, the Grimscales matching their pace alongside them. Elara could hear the sound of soldiers shouting behind them, their footsteps getting closer and closer.

"Captain Ren, we need you!" a guard shouted and somehow Elara knew just who this 'Captain Ren' was. He was the man who had sapped the magic from not just the Grimscales, but the three of them too. By all accounts, this was a very dangerous man.

"We have to split up!" Rylan yelled, his voice barely audible over the sound of their pounding feet. "You know where to go!"

Elara didn't want to split up, she felt in her heart that if they were to split up now, then it could be the very last time they would see each other. But she knew that Rylan was right. They needed to increase their chances of getting away. With a nod to Rylan, she and Kaelin took off in one direction, followed by the Grimscales, while Rylan headed in another.

Elara could hear the sound of soldiers still chasing after them, but she didn't look back. She focused all of her energy on running as fast as she could, pushing herself to her limits.

As they ran through the forest, branches and leaves slapped against their faces and bodies, but they didn't slow down. The Grimscales ran with them, their powerful legs propelling them forward effortlessly. Elara could feel the adrenaline pumping through her veins as she ran, her heart pounding in her chest. She could hear Kaelin panting beside her, but neither of them stopped. They had to keep going, keep running until they were safe.

Then Elara felt it. The mana within her receded and curled up into nothingness and she felt empty inside. Goosebumps covered her skin and a cold sweat covered her entire body in a moment. Then she saw that both the Grimscales had stopped and lay on the ground as though they were terrified into petrification.

Elara came to a stop and turned around to face the Grimscales. She could see that they were quivering with fear and their eyes were wide with panic. She reached out a hand towards them, trying to calm them down, but it was as though they didn't even see her. They were completely consumed by their fear.

"What's going on?" Kaelin asked, coming to a stop beside Elara.

"I don't know," Elara replied, her voice trembling. "My mana... it's gone again."

Kaelin's eyes widened in shock. "So has mine… do you think…"

Elara wanted to run, but before she could even think about leaving the Grimscales behind, a figure walked casually through the treeline behind the two creatures. It was the same man who they had already seen do *something* to rid the area of magic. This was unmistakably Captain Ren.

Elara felt a shiver run down her spine at the sight of the unknown entity. She could feel the fear creeping up on her once again, but she tried to stay calm and composed. She had to do whatever she could to protect Kaelin and the Grimscales, but no other soldiers appeared and if she was going to do anything, this could be her one and only chance.

"Who are you?" she asked, trying to sound brave and confident.

Captain Ren stopped a few feet away from them and looked at Elara with a mixture of amusement and contempt. "I'm the one in charge here," he said, his voice cold and flat.

"What do you want with us? And with these two?" Kaelin asked, gesturing to the Grimscales and her voice trembling slightly.

Captain Ren took a step closer to them. "I want you to know your place, earth mage," he said, his voice low and threatening. "Magic is an abomination. Outlawed by our King and as such, it carries the highest penalty of all. You should know that by now, shouldn't you?"

Elara felt a surge of anger rise up within her at Captain Ren's words. He could only have been talking about the Headmaster's impending execution.

"We're not afraid of you," Elara said, her voice steadying.

Captain Ren chuckled darkly. "We'll see about that," he said, before clicking his tongue.

As if on cue, several soldiers emerged from the treeline, their weapons drawn and pointed at Elara, Kaelin, and the Grimscales. Elara's heart pounded in her chest as she took a step back. She could feel the fear and panic rising within her again, but she refused to let it overtake her. She had to stay strong, for herself, for Kaelin, and for the creatures she needed to protect.

"What do you want from us?" Kaelin screamed.

Captain Ren sneered at her. "We want you to pay for your crimes," he said, gesturing to the Grimscales. "And we want to make an example out of you, to show others that magic will not be tolerated in our kingdom."

Elara could feel the weight of Captain Ren's words settle heavily upon her shoulders. She knew that they were in grave danger, and that their situation was rapidly becoming more and more dire. But she refused to give up. She refused to let Captain Ren and his soldiers break her spirit.

"We'll protect these creatures, and ourselves, no matter the cost."

Captain Ren's expression darkened. "Very well," he said, his voice low and dangerous. "You've made your choice. Now you'll have to face the consequences."

Elara willed her mana to return to her, to grow from the seed within but whatever she tried, no matter how hard she internally begged, there was simply nothing.

"Pathetic," Captain Ren scoffed as he evidently felt Elara's attempt to rouse her mana from within.

Then a shout came from the side of the group and charging directly at the Captain, Rylan appeared with his wooden sword held high.

"Ah, a little stronger, this one," the Captain said loudly. "But not strong enough."

Then as Elara watched, the sword within Rylan's hands abruptly shrunk down into nothing before disappearing entirely, and two soldiers appeared between Rylan and the Captain, and took a hold of his arms before he could reach his target.

"Get your hands off me!" Rylan shouted as he struggled against the guards. It was no use though and without his magic to aid him, Elara could see that Rylan was fighting a losing battle.

Then Captain Ren took a step forward towards Rylan.

"What did you really think was going to happen here?" He asked with a sly grin on his face. "Surely you did not expect to disrupt an entire camp of the kingdom's soldiers?"

Rylan glared at Captain Ren, his jaw clenched. "I expected to do what was right," he said through gritted teeth.

Captain Ren chuckled darkly. "What's right is following the law, boy. Magic is forbidden in our kingdom, and those who practice it must be punished."

Elara felt a surge of anger and frustration rise up within her. She couldn't believe that this was happening, that they had been caught and that they were now at the mercy of this ruthless Captain and his soldiers. But she refused to give up. She had to keep fighting, keep struggling, no matter the cost.

As she looked around, Elara saw movement in the trees, and then, to her surprise, A third large Grimscale appeared out of nowhere. It was larger than the other two and the largest she had ever seen by far. Something looked sleeker about this one though, more streamlined somehow. Then it hit her, this Grimscale was a female.

The soldiers, caught off guard by the beast's sudden appearance, hesitated for a moment before regaining their composure and raising their weapons.

But the Grimscale was too quick for them. It charged forward with incredible speed, its claws and beak tearing through the soldiers like a hot knife through butter. The battle was short but fierce, and within moments, the female Grimscale had dispatched most of the soldiers. Captain Ren though, had been watching motionless with a look of amusement on his face.

The two soldiers who had held Rylan had also gone, lost to the fight against the Grimscale but Rylan still stood motionless, unsure of what he was supposed to do next.

Elara ran over to Rylan, grabbing his arm and pulling him towards her. "Come on, we have to go," she said urgently.

"I don't think so," Captain Ren said without turning his head. "Let me just deal with this, and I'll be back with you in a second."

The Captain then shut his eyes and Elara felt a familiar pulse of energy beginning to exude from his body. She still had no sense of the mana within her and she knew that this new Grimscale was about to face the same fate as the other two if she didn't do anything. There was nothing she could do though.

Then almost in the blink of an eye, the father Grimscale launched itself past Elara and straight into the Captain as he weaved his mana-dispelling technique. As the beast crashed into him, Elara felt that his aura flickered and cracked and her mana immediately returned. She locked eyes with Rylan and knew that he had felt it too.

Captain Ren had been thrown across the clearing and had impacted a wide tree with a loud thud, and to Elara's surprise, the three Grimscales did not decide to end the man where he lay slumped, rather they regrouped slowly and appeared to greet each other lovingly.

Elara could hardly believe what had just happened. She felt her mana returning to her in full force, and the Grimscales appeared to be unharmed. She looked over at Rylan, who was staring at her with a mix of shock and awe.

"What just happened?" he asked, his voice barely above a whisper.

Elara shook her head, still trying to process everything. "I don't know," she replied. "But I think... I think we just witnessed something incredible."

The Grimscales began to move towards Elara, Kaelin, Rylan, and then stopped before them as though awaiting instruction.

Elara looked at the Grimscales, marvelling at their loyalty and bravery. She realised that they were waiting for her to give them an order. She looked around, trying to assess the situation. The soldiers lay motionless on the ground, and Captain Ren was nowhere to be seen. They had to move quickly, before any more soldiers arrived.

"Follow us," Elara said firmly, motioning for the Grimscales to follow her, Kaelin, and Rylan. "We need to get out of here before more soldiers arrive."

"Did you see what happened to that Captain?" Rylan asked. "I think it might have been better to just kill him."

Elara shook her head. "We can't stoop to their level," she said firmly. "We have to be better than them, no matter what."

Rylan couldn't help but agree, and they started moving quickly through the forest, with the Grimscales following closely behind. They had to be cautious and move silently, but they also had to move quickly, before any more soldiers arrived.

Elara couldn't believe her luck. They had been saved by the very creatures they had come to rescue. After a short while, she turned to Rylan, a smile spreading across her face. "We did it," she said, her voice filled with joy and relief.

Rylan grinned back at her, his eyes shining with pride. "We did," he said. "And we couldn't have done it without them." He gestured to the Grimscales, who were now standing protectively around them in their own campsite.

Elara nodded in agreement. "We owe them everything," she said, reaching out to touch the father Grimscale on the nose. "Thank you."

The Grimscale looked at her with its large, red eyes, and let out a low rumble.

Chapter 17: Distractions

A moment after the new arrivals had been assessed by the Grimscale Elara had named 'Grey', and were deemed non-threatening, two more of the creatures appeared from behind the group and walked slowly towards them. One a larger, sleepier looking version and one very clearly a juvenile. It kind of looked cute to Anya, who immediately wanted to pet it. Landon looked apprehensive.

Elara stepped forward, holding her hand out in a calming gesture. "It's okay," she said softly. "They're friends. They won't hurt us."

The male Grimscale, or Grey, approached her, its movements slow and deliberate. It nuzzled its snout against her hand, as if in greeting. This was the first time that Elara had actually touched one of the beasts, and was shocked to note that although it looked like a terribly dangerous creature, it was actually rather soft, and warm.

The juvenile Grimscale, meanwhile, seemed curious about the new arrivals. It chirped and cooed as it approached, hopping towards Anya with its eyes wide and full of wonder. Anya couldn't resist reaching out to pet it, and to her surprise, the larger Grimscales although they kept a watchful eye over their child, allowed her to do so. Anya too found its half-feathers, half-scales warm and velvety under her fingertips.

Landon watched with a mix of amazement and trepidation, unsure of what to make of the creatures. "Are these really Grimscales? I mean, how?" he asked, his voice low.

Elara nodded, still petting Grey. "Yes," she said. "These are amazing creatures. They helped us escape from the soldiers."

Landon looked at her, his expression softening. "I can see that," he said. "I'm glad you had them to help."

Anya looked up at Landon, her eyes shining. "They're so cool," she said. "Can we stay and play with them?"

Landon hesitated, but then he nodded. "I suppose we can take a little break," he said, smiling at her. "But we can't stay too long. We have so much to do."

Anya beamed, her excitement evident. "Thank you!" she said, before turning back to the Grimscale and continuing to pet it.

"What did you learn in the city?" Rylan asked, trying to bring the conversation back on track after he brought Anya and Landon up to speed on what had happened in the forest, and with Captain Ren.

"We found out that they're transferring the Headmaster to the palace tomorrow so he's ready for the big execution. Apparently it's a big deal because he's such a high-profile mage," Anya explained. "And they really hate mages in the city, and there are soldiers everywhere…"

Elara nodded. "We need to come up with a plan," she said, her mind racing with possibilities. "We can't just let them execute the Headmaster without a fight."

Rylan looked thoughtful. "I may have an idea," he said slowly. "But it's risky."

Landon raised an eyebrow. "What is it?" he asked.

"Well… if the head is being transferred *to* the palace," he said slowly, as though he was still trying to concoct the plan as he spoke. "Then maybe most of the soldiers will be concentrated around where he's being held in the meantime, then during the transfer, which will no doubt be a spectacle. In any case what I'm trying to say is…"

"The palace won't be guarded!" Elara said with wide eyes and a huge grin on her face.

"Exactly!" Rylan said. "If we get into the palace before the transfer, then maybe we can free the Headmaster before the execution, and where all the guards will be concentrating on keeping people out, we can make our escape."

Landon looked skeptical. "That's a lot of 'maybes'," he said, crossing his arms. "And even if it does work, how are we supposed to get into the palace undetected?"

Rylan shrugged. "I'm still working on that part," he admitted.

"Ah I knew it was too good to be true," Kaelin said loudly.

"What?" Rylan asked, "It's a good plan for the most part, isn't it?"

"It is, but I mean it's too good to be true that you would come up with a half-decent plan all the way through, all by yourself, stick boy." She smiled broadly and her statement made Elara let out a little snort.

Rylan rolled his eyes. "Ha ha, very funny," he said sarcastically. "But at least I'm trying to come up with something."

Kaelin held up her hands in surrender. "Okay, okay, I'm sorry," she said. "But you have to admit, it's not exactly foolproof."

Elara spoke up, her mind racing. "Maybe it won't be so difficult to sneak into the palace," she said. "Maybe we can create a distraction nearby, and because there will be less guards around, they'll leave the place pretty much unguarded? Then we can practically walk right through the front door and await the arrival of the Headmaster."

Landon looked at her, his expression thoughtful. "That could work," he said slowly. "But what kind of distraction?"

Elara's eyes gleamed with excitement. "I have an idea," she said, a smile spreading across her face. "A really big one." She gave a sideways glance to the three Grimscales that were still watching the group. It looked as though they were listening intently, and even understood the conversation, though there was no way of knowing if that was the case or not.

Elara looked at the Grimscales, her mind racing with possibilities. "What if we used the Grimscales to create a distraction?" she said. "They're incredibly fast and strong, and they could easily crash through the city gates, run through the city, and create chaos. While everyone is distracted, we could slip inside the palace."

Rylan looked impressed. "That's actually not a bad idea," he said. "But how do we control the Grimscales? We can't just let them loose and hope for the best."

Elara nodded, understanding his concern. "Maybe we could just try asking them?" then her eyes fell upon the baby Grimscale, and she regretted having voiced the plan at all. She couldn't expect this little family to put themselves in danger for them.

But to Elara's surprise, the father Grimscale stepped forward, its large red eyes focused on her. It let out a low rumble, and Elara felt a jolt of electricity run through her. She knew, somehow, that the Grimscale was agreeing to her plan.

Anya looked up at the Grimscales, her eyes wide with excitement. "Oh, can we ride them?" she asked with a hopeful expression on her face.

Elara looked at Anya, then back at the Grimscales. "I really don't think so," she said. "They're not just animals, they're intelligent creatures with their own lives and families."

Rylan nodded, his expression serious. "Agreed," he said. "We'll use them as a distraction, but we won't put them in any unnecessary danger."

Landon looked at the Grimscales, then back at the group. "Seriously?" he asked.

"For the Headmaster, and for all the other mages who are being persecuted by the King we can do this," Elara replied.

The group fell into a thoughtful silence, each lost in their own thoughts about the plan. Finally, Kaelin spoke up.

"So, how do we make it happen?" she asked.

Elara looked at the Grimscales again, considering. "We'll need to coordinate with them somehow," she said. "And we'll need to time it just right."

Rylan nodded. "And we'll need to move quickly," he said. "Once the distraction is set, we'll have a limited amount of time before the guards catch on."

Landon took a deep breath, his expression determined. "OK, let's do it," he said, his eyes meeting Elara's.

"But there's one more thing that we aren't accounting for…" Anya said slowly. "What about Captain Ren, and the others like him that seem to be able to suppress magic, and to capture the Grimscales?"

The group fell silent, considering Anya's question. Elara spoke up after a moment.

"We'll have to be careful and stay alert," she said. "We can't let them catch us off guard, and we'll have to be ready to fight if necessary."

"Agreed," Rylan said. "We can't take any chances."

Kaelin looked at the Grimscales again, her expression contemplative.

"And we need to make sure that they're safe," she said. "We can't just use them and leave them to the soldiers."

Elara replied in a serious tone: "We'll make sure that they're taken care of," she said. "We owe them that much."

Then she turned to the father Grimscale, Grey as she had named him and spoke in a soft, hushed tone.

"Can you understand me?" She asked.

We won't let anything happen to you or your family," she said. "We'll make sure you're safe."

Grey looked at Elara for a moment, then let out a low rumble, as if in agreement. Elara took it as a sign that he understood her, and she felt a sense of relief.

"Our plan is to create a distraction at the city gates so that we can all get inside without the soldiers taking too much notice of us. We need to save our friend inside the palace, but we can't get inside without your help."

Grey seemed to listen to Elara's words with keen interest, his head bobbing side to side. He looked towards the city gates and then back at Elara, as if assessing the situation. Elara held her breath, wondering if Grey would agree to help them. After a few tense moments, Grey let out another low rumble, which Elara took as a sign of affirmation.

"Then I guess the only thing left, is to give a name to this cute little guy," Anya said, and Elara noticed that the Master-ranked mage was now on her knees, trying to get the baby Grimscale to come to her as though it was some sort of cat.

"Oh, how about Little Rylan?" Kaelin said with a smile and the rest of the group – except Rylan himself – laughed merrily.

Rylan rolled his eyes good-naturedly at the suggestion but couldn't help a small smile from creeping onto his lips. "How about we give him a name that's not related to me?" he said with a chuckle.

Anya grinned mischievously. "How about Spark?" she suggested. "Because he's so full of energy and electricity."

"Is he?" Landon asked, looking at the little guy and knowing full-well the baby Grimscale had barely moved since the first time he and Anya had seen it.

Elara nodded, liking the name. "Spark it is," she said. "And we'll make sure he's safe along with the rest of his family during the distraction."

Rylan looked at Elara with admiration. "You have a way with animals," he said. "I'm impressed."

Elara felt a blush creep onto her cheeks at his compliment. "It's nothing special," she said, trying to play it off.

Landon cleared his throat, interrupting the moment. "As much as I'd love to stay and chat about cute baby Grimscales, we should probably get moving," he said. "We don't want to miss our chance to rescue the Headmaster."

"Right," Rylan said. "But first, Elara, could we have a quick word in private before we go?"

Elara felt her heart race at Rylan's request, wondering what he wanted to talk to her about in private. She nodded hesitantly, feeling a mix of excitement and nervousness. The rest of the group nodded and gave them space as they walked a few steps away from the Grimscales.

Once they were alone, Rylan turned to Elara, his expression serious. "I just wanted to say that I appreciate your bravery, and everything you've done for us," he said. "You're an incredible mage and an even better person. I'm glad to have you on our team."

Elara felt a warmth spread through her at Rylan's words, and she couldn't help but smile. "Thank you, Rylan," she said. "I feel the same way about you. You're a great leader too, and I couldn't ask for a better teammate."

Rylan's eyes softened as he looked at Elara, and for a moment, there was a tense silence between them.

"I want you to have this," he blurted out quickly, handing Elara the locket from his father that he had lent her before to practise her mana with."

"I… I can't take that," she hesitated, her eyes wide.

Rylan shook his head, insisting. "Please, Elara. I want you to have it. It's important to me that you keep it safe."

Elara looked at the locket in her hand, feeling overwhelmed by the gesture. She knew how much the locket meant to Rylan, and she couldn't believe he was just giving it to her. "I'll keep it safe," she said, her voice barely above a whisper.

Rylan smiled at her, his eyes meeting hers. "I know you will," he said. "And I trust you."

Elara felt a flutter in her stomach at his words, realising just how much she cared about Rylan. She had been so focused on their mission and saving the Headmaster that she hadn't allowed herself to think about her feelings for him. But in that moment, with Rylan looking at her with such trust and admiration, she couldn't deny the way her heart raced at the thought of him.

They stood there for a moment longer, lost in their own thoughts, before Rylan quickly leant forward and kissed Elara on the cheek.

Shocked, she couldn't say a single word before Landon's voice interrupted them. "Guys, we need to move. Now."

Rylan and Elara nodded, snapping out of their trance. They re-joined the group and made their way towards the city gates, with Grey and his family by their side. As they approached, Elara felt her nerves kick in, knowing that everything was riding on their success. She looked at Rylan, and he gave her a reassuring nod.

As the gates came into clear view, suddenly, Grey and his family burst forward, running towards the gates at an incredible speed. The soldiers were caught off guard, and they stumbled backwards as the Grimscales immediately crashed into them.

Elara watched in amazement at the stupidity of the two guards as they moved away from the gates to engage the three Grimscales. Though, perhaps it wasn't stupidity, as the beasts were particularly frightening, and they were standing off the guards whilst snapping their beaks at them.

Spark also snapped his little beak at the guards, though his parents did a good job of standing between him and the guards to keep him safe.

"Now!" Rylan said to the others, and they all slipped through the gates whilst the three Grimscales caused their distraction.

As soon as they had made it inside, a warning bell started to ring, and a stream of guards began running towards the gates and the Grimscales.

Elara's heart dropped for a moment seeing how many guards were going to join the fight, but with a glance backwards, she saw the three creatures turn and run towards the forest, followed by all of the guards, who were determined to try to keep up with them.

Elara breathed a sigh of relief as the Grimscales and the guards disappeared into the distance. It was a risky move, but it had worked. They had made it inside the city without being caught. And the Grimscales had been invaluable in their help, but had also managed to escape too.

Rylan turned to the group. "We need to move quickly," he said. "The guard at the palace will be minimal right now; it's our best chance to get inside."

They all nodded in reply and followed Rylan as he began to lead them through the winding streets of the city. It was chaotic, with people running in every direction and the few guards that remained tried to keep order. It seemed that word of Grimscales at the gates had reached the city almost immediately and had caused widespread panic. Their plan had worked better than they could've expected.

Elara pulled her hood over her head and kept her gaze low, so nobody would be able to see the shimmering green of the mana within her eyes.

Chapter 18: Hiding Place

The group moved through the city streets slowly so they would not bring any unnecessary attention to themselves. Just as soon as they thought they had been making progress though, they heard a stern voice not too far ahead of them command: "Open your eyes."

Elara's heart sank. If the guards were still taking the time to check to see if any mages were present, she didn't know how they were going to be able to make it through to the palace.

Just as she pondered though, a strong hand grabbed her arm and pulled her off to the side and away from the busy street.

Elara stumbled for a moment before regaining her balance and turning to face her saviour. It was Landon, his expression serious as he gestured for the rest of the group to follow them.

They followed Landon through a narrow alleyway, away from the main streets and the prying eyes of the guards. As they walked, Elara couldn't help but feel grateful for Landon's quick thinking and his ability to keep them all safe.

Finally, they emerged from the alleyway and found themselves in a small square with a few rundown buildings and a fountain in the centre. Landon led them to one of the buildings, which appeared to be abandoned, and gestured for them to follow him inside.

The inside of the building was dimly lit, and the air was musty with the smell of dust and disuse. Landon led them to a room at the back of the building and gestured for them to take a seat on the floor.

"We should be safe here for now," he said, his voice low. "But we can't stay here for too long. The guards will no doubt be searching the city for anything suspicious."

Rylan nodded. "We need to find a way to get to the palace," he said. "But we have to be quick. Most of the guards are chasing our friends in the forest, and we'll never get another chance like this."

"We'll just wait here for a little while until the guards are a little less jumpy," Kaelin said matter-of-factly. "They probably only came out because the people are going nuts because of the Grimscales. We'll give it five minutes, then get back onto the road."

Elara looked around the dusty room, feeling restless. She knew they didn't have much time, and every second counted. "We can't wait too long," she said, her voice urgent. "We need to move as soon as possible."

"Elara's right," Rylan said. "We don't have time to waste. We need to get to the palace before the guards realise what's happening.'

They all fell silent, lost in thought as they contemplated their next move. After a few minutes, Rylan stood up, his eyes resolute. "Alright, let's do this," he said. "We're going to have to be smart and work together. We can do this."

Elara felt a surge of adrenaline wash over her as the group left the abandoned house and moved back towards the main roads, and thankfully, Kaelin had been right; there were far fewer people about now and not a single guard to be seen. It was almost like order had been restored, and it was business as usual again. She spared a thought for Grey and his family, hoping that they escaped without any issues.

The group moved quickly and quietly through the city streets, their cloaks billowing behind them. Elara kept her gaze low, trying to avoid drawing attention to herself. The palace loomed in the distance, its grandeur overwhelming. Elara couldn't help but feel a sense of awe mixed with fear at the thought of what lay inside.

Two guards stood at the gates to the palace, and a high stone wall spanned its perimeter to keep anyone out who shouldn't be there. Beyond the gates though, Elara could not see a single guard patrolling the interior grounds.

"This way," Rylan said, leading the group around to the left of the gates. Then after a short while tracing the high wall, he extended his hands to the wall, and thick vines began to silently extend from the ground and snaked their way up the wall until they reached the top.

His magic was beautiful, and again Elara felt inadequate with the small control she had over her own mana.

The group climbed up the vines and onto the top of the wall, careful not to make any noise. From there, they could see the empty palace gardens below them, and they quickly descended the vines on the far side of the wall to land softly on the ground before anyone could see them if they took too long.

The gardens were deserted, and the only sound was the gentle rustling of leaves in the breeze.

Elara couldn't help but gasp in amazement at the sight before her. The palace grounds were stunningly beautiful, with perfectly manicured gardens filled with colourful flowers and carefully trimmed hedges. Small fountains and statues dotted the landscape, adding to the ambiance of the already picturesque surroundings.

In the centre of the gardens stood a massive stone fountain, its water cascading down several tiers and reflecting the light of the sun in a shimmering dance. Beyond the gardens, Elara could see the palace itself, a grand structure made of white marble with intricately carved pillars and archways.

The palace gleamed in the sunlight, looking almost ethereal in its beauty. Elara couldn't help but feel a sense of reverence at the thought of being in the presence of such grandeur and opulence. The palace was truly a sight to behold, and Elara couldn't help but feel grateful for the opportunity to see it with her own eyes.

As they moved closer to the palace, Elara noticed something that made her blood run cold. In the midst of the beautiful gardens, there was a gallows set up, its wooden structure looming ominously over the lush greenery. The platform was empty, but it was clear that it was meant for the Headmaster's execution.

Elara felt a wave of sadness wash over her as she thought about the fate that awaited the kind and wise Headmaster. She knew they had to act fast if they wanted to save him.

Rylan seemed to notice her distress and put a reassuring hand on her shoulder. "We'll get him out of there," he said, determination in his voice.

Elara nodded, feeling grateful for Rylan's confidence. They continued to make their way through the gardens, their eyes peeled for any signs of guards or obstacles in their path. They passed by carefully manicured hedges, fountains with ornate sculptures, and flower beds bursting with vibrant colours. Despite the looming threat of danger, Elara couldn't help but continue to appreciate the beauty of the palace grounds.

As they approached the entrance to the palace, Elara's heart began to race. This was it, the moment they had been waiting for. They had to find the Headmaster and get him out of there as quickly as possible.

Rylan gestured for the group to stay back as he approached a large wooden door and listened carefully. After a moment, he turned back to them and shook his head. "It's locked," he whispered.

Elara felt a sense of panic rise within her. They couldn't fail now, not after coming so far. She turned to the group, trying to think of a plan.

"We need to find another way in," she said, her voice low. "There has to be another entrance."

Kaelin nodded. "There's a side entrance on the left side of the palace. It's for the servants to come and go, so it might not be locked."

"Then that's our way in," Rylan said, determination in his voice. "Let's move."

The group quickly made their way towards the side entrance, staying low and trying to avoid being seen. As they approached, Elara's nerves kicked in again. They were so close to finding the Headmaster, but they were also so close to being caught. There would be no explaining their way out of this one.

Kaelin motioned for them to stop as they neared the side entrance. "There might be guards inside, so we need to be careful," she warned.

Rylan nodded and took a deep breath before slowly pushing the door open. They stepped inside, their eyes scanning the area for any sign of guards. The room was dimly lit, with only a few candles casting a flickering light around the space. The air was heavy with the scent of perfume and cleaning supplies.

They made their way through the winding corridors, staying low and moving quickly. The palace was labyrinthine, with countless twists and turns that seemed designed to disorientate intruders.

As they approached a large set of double doors, they heard voices on the other side. They didn't sound official or distressed though, so perhaps these were the voices of some of the servants.

Rylan motioned for the group to stay back as he slowly pushed the doors open, revealing a large chamber with a high ceiling and walls adorned with tapestries and paintings. In the centre of the room stood a man and a woman, speaking nonchalantly.

Elara's heart rose, then sank as she recognised the pair. It was her parents.

They were deep in conversation, seemingly oblivious to the group's presence. Elara wanted to rush forward and embrace them, but she knew that they couldn't risk being caught. She signalled to the group to stay back and watch from a distance.

Elara watched her parents for a moment, feeling a strange mix of emotions. On one hand, she was overjoyed to see them alive and well. On the other hand, she knew that either they had been enlisted as slaves, or had finally been unable to pay their debts to the city, and had been forced to work them off instead.

Her heart sank as she realised the latter was more likely. She knew how much her parents struggled to make ends meet and how they often fell short on their payments to the crown. It was a cruel fate, but unfortunately, not uncommon in the city. What was worse was the feeling Elara had that this was all her fault. If she hadn't had her mana awakened and had to flee, would she have been able to put in more hours on the farm? She felt tears begin to fill her eyes and had to wipe them away with her fingers.

Elara shook her thoughts away and watched them for a few more moments, trying to figure out their situation. Were they in danger? Did they need her help? She wanted to approach them and ask, but she knew it was too risky. They had to remain unnoticed, or it would be the death of them all. At least her parents looked well, and they were together.

She turned to Rylan and the others, gesturing for them to follow her as they silently slipped back out of the room and continued down the corridors. As they moved deeper into the palace, the tension in the air grew thicker. They could hear voices and footsteps echoing through the halls, but they couldn't tell if they were coming from guards or servants and sometimes the sounds seemed to echo all around them.

Finally, they reached another large set of double doors, but this time they were guarded by two heavily armed soldiers. Elara's heart raced as she realised that this was likely where the Headmaster was going to be held once he was transferred to the palace.

It was strange, she could see the two guards, but their presence made Elara feel like things had just got a lot more dangerous. The palace had been empty as yet, but having a door guarded meant at least they were surely in the right place.

The group moved back along the corridor they had arrived from and slowly opened the first small, non-imposing door they came to.

The group slipped inside and quietly closed the door behind themselves.

Once they were all inside and the door was closed, Anya turned to Rylan. "What do we do now?" she asked, her voice low.

Rylan looked lost in thought for a moment. In truth, he hadn't thought that there would be guards at the door to the room where the Headmaster would be held – especially if he hadn't yet arrived.

Then it hit him.

"They'll move to collect the Headmaster when he arrives and bring him to the room, won't they?"

"We wait," he said. "We'll stay hidden here and wait until the guards move away to collect the Headmaster. Then, we slip inside the room."

"But what if they don't move?" Landon asked with a concerned look on his face. "What if they just wait there and the other soldiers just bring him along?"

"Why don't you suggest another distraction?" Anya said with a smile.

"Nah," Rylan said. "The other guards will probably stay outside and stand guard in case anyone tries to enact a daring rescue."

Elara nodded, relieved that they had a plan and that it at least had a small chance of success. If the guards didn't leave, then they would have to come up with something else and fast. They settled into the small room, trying to make themselves as comfortable as possible. They couldn't afford to be restless, as any noise could alert the guards outside.

Then Elara couldn't hold it in any longer.

"The two servants we saw earlier… they were my parents," she blurted out.

Rylan looked at Elara, first with surprise, then understanding. "I'm sorry," he said softly. "That must have been hard for you."

Elara nodded, tears welling up in her eyes again. "I'm just glad they're alive," she said. "But I don't know what their situation is, and I couldn't risk approaching them."

"We'll figure it out," Kaelin said reassuringly. "Once we get the Headmaster out of here, we can try to help your parents too."

Rylan then slumped down on the ground beside Elara and wrapped an arm around her.

"We're all in this together," he said. "I promise we'll do everything we can to help your parents and the Headmaster. At least they aren't in any danger though, right?"

Elara shook her head. "I don't know," she said. "My parents are working as servants in the palace, and the Headmaster is set to be executed on the gallows in the gardens... it seems like all there is around here is danger."

Rylan's grip on Elara tightened as he listened to her words. He couldn't imagine the fear and anxiety that she must be feeling at that moment, knowing that her parents were in a precarious situation and that the Headmaster's life was at risk. But he knew that they couldn't afford to let their emotions get the better of them. They had a mission to complete, and they needed to focus on that.

"Right now, all we can do is stay hidden and wait for our chance," Rylan said, his voice calm and steady. "We'll get the Headmaster out of here, and then we'll figure out what to do about your parents."

Elara nodded, feeling grateful for Rylan's reassuring presence. She leaned into him slightly, finding comfort in his warmth and strength. The group settled into a tense silence, waiting for their chance to make their move.

After what felt like hours, they heard the sound of footsteps approaching the door. Rylan tensed, and the rest of the group held their breath, waiting for the guards to move away. They listened as the footsteps grew louder, and then suddenly, they stopped outside the door. The group continued to hold their breath, waiting for the worst.

But after a few tense moments, the footsteps moved away, and the group let out a collective sigh of relief. They waited a few more minutes to make sure the guards were truly gone before making their move.

Rylan motioned for the group to follow him, and they quietly slipped out of the small room and into the corridor. They moved swiftly and silently, their hearts pounding with adrenaline. As they approached the now unguarded door, they could hear nothing but silence inside. Rylan motioned for the group to get into position, and they readied themselves for what was to come.

With a deep breath, Rylan pushed open the door, and the group slipped silently inside.

The empty room was large and circular, with tall windows that let in the moonlight. In the centre of the room, there was a raised platform with a set of stairs leading up to it. And on the platform sat an empty chair that could only have been readied for the arrival of the Headmaster.

"This is definitely the place," Rylan whispered. "All we have to do now, is find somewhere good to hide, and await the arrival of the Headmaster in a few minutes."

The group spread out, searching for a suitable hiding spot. Elara's heart raced as she scanned the room, trying to find a good place to conceal themselves. She noticed a large tapestry hanging on the wall opposite the platform that reached all the way down to the ground and gestured towards it, and the group hurried over to the tapestry, slipping behind it, taking care not to make a sound.

They waited in tense silence, their ears straining for any sound of approaching guards. Elara couldn't help but worry about the safety of her parents and the Headmaster. She hoped that they were alright and that they would be able to make it out of the palace safely.

Then the doors that led into the room burst open and the sound of clanging chains, armour and footsteps rang out. There were a few strained muffles and a man ordered someone to 'sit', but after a minute or so, the sound of people leaving again was evident, and the room was quiet again, save for the tiny sound of a single person with laboured breathing.

The group stayed hidden behind the tapestry, waiting for the sound of the guards to fade away completely before making their move. Finally, they heard the doors close with a loud thud, and the room fell silent once again.

Rylan motioned for the group to follow him, and they cautiously made their way towards the platform. As they approached, they could see the Headmaster sitting on the chair, his hands bound tightly behind him in thick shackles with heavy looking chains attached to them. He looked tired and defeated as though he had been beaten, but his eyes lit up when he saw the group.

"You have no idea how pleasant it is to see friendly faces," he said in a tone that betrayed exhaustion. "Even if you look like you are all about to vomit through anxiety."

"We got your message," Elara whispered. "And we're here to set you free."

As Elara spoke, Rylan quickly moved to try to undo the chains that bound Master Arin to the chair but after a moment, he began to look frustrated, shaking his head.

The Headmaster met Elara's eyes but he did not look hopeful, rather to Elara he seemed full of apologetic sorrow.

"I can see that the Academy has served you well," Master Arin said. "But I am afraid that my freedom is not something that is on the cards for us now. I have known for some time that this is to be my end, and I tell you this now so that you do not suffer the same fate as me."

The group looked at each other in shock and confusion, not fully understanding what the Headmaster was saying. Rylan stepped forward. "What do you mean, Master Arin? We came all this way to save you. We can't just leave you here to be executed. What is with these chains though, and the lock? I can't get them to budge."

The Headmaster sighed heavily. "I appreciate your efforts, Rylan, but it's already too late for me. The shackles and chains that bind me will not be broken, and I believe that I may at least be able to do some good before I pass."

The group looked at each other, unsure of what to do. They had come all this way to save the Headmaster, and now he was saying that there was no hope for him. Elara felt a sense of despair wash over her. They had risked everything to come here, and now it seemed like it had all been for nothing.

Rylan stepped forward once again. "Master Arin, is there anything we can do? Any way we can help you?"

The Headmaster shook his head sadly. "I'm afraid not, Rylan. My fate has already been sealed. But there is something I need to tell you. Something that could help to change the course of the future once I have passed on into the care of the afterworld."

"What is it?" Kaelin asked with wide eyes.

"There is a faction within the soldiers. It seems I had underestimated the King in his desire to rid the world of magic and its users. He despises magic of course, but he is apparently not above recruiting mages to help him in his crusade."

"What?" Rylan asked incredulously. "Are you saying there are mages within the city guard?"

"That is exactly what I am saying," Master Arin replied. "There are three that I know of, all of them imbued with Cyclonic Essence…"

"They're air affinity mages?" Anya asked in shock. She was about to follow up with another question, when Elara interrupted them.

"Captain Ren," she practically whispered.

The Headmaster nodded. "He is indeed their leader, and a very powerful mage. I would say an Archmage at least, but perhaps even the Grandmaster of the air affinity himself. He is the reason that I am unable to escape, and also the reason why the creatures in the forest are being pushed from their homes."

"You know about the creatures in the forest?" Elara asked.

The Headmaster nodded. "I have always had a way with the creatures in the Forbidden Forest. You may recall that I spoke about sources of information… well, these creatures served me well as my ears and eyes while we practised in the Academy," Master Arin explained.

"But how do air affinity mages do all that?" Kaelin asked. "Don't they just make, like, wind and stuff?"

Rylan turned to face Kaelin now. "Come on, don't you know anything? Air mages are Master of space magic and illusion, they can make you see things, feel things that aren't really there."

"And they are also able to affect the presence of mana in the space around them," Arin said. "Captain Ren is especially gifted at suppressing the mana within a mage, and that is why he is the most dangerous person I have ever had the misfortune to meet. Even more dangerous than King Roderick himself, I believe."

"But why would he help them?" Rylan asked. "The King hates mages, I don't get why he would even want to use them either."

The Headmaster shook his head. "I am afraid I do not have all the answers to your questions. But take this warning with you when you leave this place: Stay away from Captain Ren."

The group remained silent for a long moment as they let all the new information seep in. Then the Headmaster turned to Elara and spoke.

"I sense you have a question for me. Please, do not feel the need to remain polite in the presence of a dying man."

Elara did in fact have a question for Master Arin. "When I saw you fight back in the woods, you used a staff to fight and then used a spell to throw the soldiers back… If you're a powerful Archmage, why didn't you do something stronger?"

Everyone seemed to be staring at Elara as though she had just grown an extra head, but nobody said anything as they awaited the Headmaster's answer. Eventually, he smiled.

"Being a powerful mage and having great control over one's mana does not give one the ability to choose the path of life or death for another. This is a good lesson to learn, and it is this simple fact that separates us all from the king; he believes that he can choose when others will perish – and in some ways he can – but if there is one thing that he cannot do, it is to escape the long, slow march that we all walk to the end of our days."

Chapter 19: Escape

Elara simply couldn't accept that there was nothing the group could do to save the Headmaster. They had tried so hard and risked so much just to get here, and he was just going to lay down and accept his fate? It made her mad and she couldn't help but feel the anger begin to boil up inside her.

She stood up, her fists clenched, and turned to face the Headmaster. "I can't just sit here and watch you die," she said, her voice trembling with emotion. "There has to be something we can do."

The Headmaster looked at Elara with a soft smile. "My dear, I appreciate your passion and your desire to help, but sometimes the best course of action is to accept our fate and make peace with it. I have lived a long and full life, and if my death can help inspire others to stand up against the tyranny of the King, then it will not have been in vain."

Elara shook her head, tears streaming down her face. "No, I can't accept that. We have to do something."

Rylan stood up beside her, placing a comforting hand on her shoulder. "Elara, he's right," he said softly. "We've done all we can. We can't risk our lives for a lost cause."

Elara looked at Rylan, then back at the Headmaster. She knew that they were both right, but she couldn't help feeling like there had to be something more they could do.

As she stood there, lost in thought, a sound caught her attention. It was the sound of footsteps echoing through the hallway outside the small room they were in. They seemed to be simply moving past so nobody made another sound until the footsteps had disappeared.

"Listen to me," Master Arin said with an urgency in his tone. "The Academy must remain safe, as must you all. Every moment you are here is a risk and you must leave right now. My life has come to an end, but you five can make changes that will shape the world we live in for years to come. Train hard and never stop fighting for what is right, but now, go. Leave me to my fate and begin to forge your own path."

Elara looked at the Headmaster, tears still streaming down her face. She knew that he was right, that they had to leave before they were caught. But the thought of leaving him there to die alone was almost unbearable.

"Thank you, Master Arin," she said, her voice choked with emotion. "We won't forget your sacrifice. And we'll do what we can to right these wrongs."

Elara, Rylan, Kaelin, Landon and Anya each placed a loving hand on their Headmaster and said their goodbyes. They would see him again, but in the morning at his public execution.

They then moved towards the large doors and Rylan opened them a crack before gesturing to the others that the coast was clear. As one, they all slipped back out into the hallway.

Once they were outside the room, they quickly made their way through the labyrinthine palace, trying to avoid being seen. The tension in the air was palpable, and the sound of their footsteps echoed loudly in the empty hallways.

Elara felt a mixture of relief and sadness. They had managed to escape, but at what cost? The Headmaster was going to be executed in the morning. And what about her parents? She still didn't know what their fate would be.

As they neared the exit, they heard voices coming from around the corner. Rylan motioned for the group to stop and stay back, as he slowly peeked around the corner to see who was there.

When he turned back to Elara, the colour had drained from his face, and he looked terrified.

"It's Captain Ren and a few soldiers," he whispered back to the group. "We need to find another way out, and fast."

But just as he spoke, the voices stopped abruptly, and Elara heard footsteps coming towards them from where the Captain and the soldiers were. The Captain must have known that they were there.

Elara's eyes widened in an instant. "RUN!" she half whispered, half shouted.

"I can sense your presence," Captain Ren's voice followed Elara's exclamation.

The group didn't need to be told twice. They took off running in the opposite direction as fast as they could, with Elara leading the way. She could hear the soldiers' footsteps getting closer and closer, and her heart felt like it was about to burst out of her chest.

As they turned a corner, they found themselves facing a dead end. They were trapped.

Elara quickly looked around, trying to find a way out. Then she spotted a small window high up on the wall.

"Up there!" she shouted, pointing to the window. "We can climb out."

Without hesitation, Rylan and Kaelin boosted Landon up to the window and he then helped the others climb up and follow him out.

As they dropped down to the other side, Elara saw that they were in a small courtyard, surrounded by tall walls. There was no way out, except for the large gate that led back into the palace.

"We have to make a run for it," Rylan said, taking the lead once again. "Stay close and keep moving."

The group burst through the gate and into the open air, sprinting as fast as they could towards the nearest alleyway. They could hear the soldiers' shouts and footsteps behind them, getting closer by the second.

Just as they were about to reach the alley, a hand reached out from a nearby doorway and grabbed Elara's arm, pulling her inside. Turning to see what had happened, the group all followed Elara through the door to do whatever they could to help her.

Elara was being held with a hand covering her mouth to keep her silent and as she watched the rest of the group enter the dark room with wide eyes, she saw that Rylan had conjured his wooden sword and held it menacingly towards Elara's captors.

The captor, a middle-aged woman with a determined expression on her face, held up her hands in surrender, letting Elara go to stand with her friends. "Please, we're not your enemies," she said, her voice barely above a whisper. "We saw you being chased, and we wanted to help."

Rylan lowered his sword slightly, eyeing the woman suspiciously. "Who are you?"

"My name is Sariel," she said. "I'm part of a resistance group here in the city. We've been trying to overthrow the King's regime for years. "

"What can we do to help?" Elara asked, a flame of hope igniting within her.

Sariel looked at the group, sizing them up. "You look capable," she said. "But it is not the time right now. You must leave this place and return one day when the time is right."

Elara's heart sank at Sariel's words. She had been hoping that perhaps they had a new chance to free the Headmaster, but it seemed that again, luck was not on their side.

"When will the time be right?" Kaelin asked, her voice full of frustration. "The Headmaster is going to be executed tomorrow if we don't do anything!"

Sariel shook her head. "I know," she said. "But I promise you, you will know when the time comes, everyone will. For now, you must leave the city, get back to whatever safety you came from and keep yourselves safe."

The group exchanged glances, uncertain of what to do next. They had risked everything to come this far, and now they were being told to leave and wait for a future that might never come.

But deep down, Elara knew that Sariel was right. They were too inexperienced and too few to take on the King's army. With Captain Ren, too, they had no hope of even trying to fight. They needed to leave and regroup, to come back stronger and more prepared.

"My parents…" Elara said after a moment of silence. "They're working for the King as servants…"

Sariel's expression softened. "I understand," she said. 'But for now, you need to focus on getting out of the city safely. We can't risk going back in for your parents right now, but we will keep an eye out for them and if they are working in the palace at least they will be safe for now."

Elara nodded thoughtfully, feeling a mix of sadness and relief. She knew that Sariel was right, and that they needed to prioritise their own safety for now. But the thought of leaving her parents behind still weighed heavily on her heart.

Sariel then turned to the group. "I can help you get out of the city safely," she said. "But we need to move quickly. The longer you stay here, the greater the risk of being caught."

The group agreed, and Sariel led them out of the small room and through a maze of hidden passages and backstreets. They moved quickly, always staying in the shadows and avoiding any guards or patrols they saw.

"Now go," Sariel ordered as they reached a main city street. "Blend into the crowds and keep your heads down."

The group nodded their thanks to Sariel and quickly merged into the throngs of people moving through the streets. They tried to blend in as best they could, but Elara couldn't help feeling like everyone was staring at them, like they knew what they had just done.

They walked in silence and Elara let her mind wander back to the Headmaster and how frightened he must've been, despite his calm demeanour.

"This way," Landon said abruptly, leading the group to one side of the street. Elara knew that it wasn't the way out of the city and before them she could see a small tavern with people both inside and out.

Elara hesitated, unsure if it was safe to stop and rest at the tavern. But Landon seemed confident, and the group was exhausted from their escape. They followed him inside, finding a small table in the corner where they could sit and rest without heading to the bar.

"What are we doing here?" Elara whispered with a fair amount of urgency in her voice. All around them, people were drinking and talking, and she didn't know how long they would be able to remain inconspicuous for.

"We owe it to the Headmaster to be nearby in his final hours," Landon said. "We can remain in the city until the morning, then attend the execution."

Landon's tone gave no hope of Elara talking him out of this course of action, but deep down, she agreed with him.

On the table in front of them were some almost empty tankards, and they each took a hold of one so that nobody would get suspicious of the fact they had no drinks.

As the night wore on, the tavern slowly emptied out and the group became more and more anxious. They knew they needed to leave before it was too late, but they didn't want to risk being caught outside.

Then with a crash, the door to the tavern suddenly opened, and a group of soldiers marched in, their weapons drawn and held to the ready. The tavern went silent. Elara's heart raced as she looked around, searching for a way out. But they were trapped.

"The Archmage will be executed in the morning!" the lead soldier announced loudly. Then after a long pause, he shouted: "Drinks for everybody!"

Elara felt a mix of relief and confusion as the soldiers ordered drinks for everyone in the tavern. It was a strange turn of events, but she knew they couldn't let their guard down.

The group tried to blend in with the other patrons, sipping their tankards after they had been placed on the table in front of them while the soldiers moved through the tavern and made idle conversation. There mood was far too happy for what they were going to do to the Headmaster though.

As the soldiers finished their drinks and eventually left the tavern, the group breathed a collective sigh of relief. But they knew that they couldn't stay there any longer.

"We need to leave now," Rylan said, standing up and motioning for the others to follow him. "It's not too cold out tonight and we don't have too long to wait."

The group quickly left the tavern and made their way back to the hidden passage that Sariel had shown them earlier. It looked as though the alleyway was seldom used and all of the students slumped down to the ground with their backs against the walls.

They sat in silence for a long time before Rylan attempted to raise the mood of the group.

"We did well tonight," Rylan said, a note of pride in his voice. "We managed to escape and avoid being caught. We even found a way to stay close to the Headmaster until the end."

Elara nodded, but she couldn't shake the feeling of sadness that had settled over her. "But at what cost?" she said quietly. "We lost the Headmaster, and I still don't know what's happening to my parents."

The group fell silent, all of them feeling the weight of their losses. It was a reminder that their fight was far from over, and that there was still so much they needed to do to bring justice to their kingdom.

"We'll find a way to make it right," Kaelin said finally, breaking the silence. "We'll make sure the Headmaster's sacrifice wasn't in vain, and we'll find a way to free your parents from the King's grasp."

Elara smiled gratefully at Kaelin. It was comforting to have such loyal friends by her side. "Thank you," she said softly.

Landon spoke up next. "We also need to find a way to connect with the resistance. If these new air mage soldiers are going around causing trouble, then it affects everyone and not just the Academy."

"We can start by reaching out to Sariel once all this is over. They must have some ideas about how to fight the King's troops or at least ways we can help other mages who remain in hiding," Rylan said.

The group silently acknowledged the importance of finding allies in their fight against the King's regime. It was clear that they couldn't do this alone, and they needed to band together with others who shared their cause.

As they sat in the quiet alleyway, each lost in their own thoughts, Elara couldn't help but feel a renewed sense of determination. They had come so far, but they still had a long way to go. They couldn't give up now, not when so much was at stake.

"We should get some rest," she said, breaking the silence. "We'll need all our strength for tomorrow."

The others agreed, and they settled down for the night, each taking turns keeping watch. Elara closed her eyes, feeling the exhaustion wash over her. The last thing she felt before she fell into slumber, was Rylan's fingers interlocking with her own as he held her hand.

Chapter 20: Execution

Elara awoke with the feeling of the warm sun on her face. The alleyway that they had slept within was mostly dark still, but the rising sun had found a way to shine a few slivers of light onto the group. Elara felt a moment of happiness before she remembered where she was, and that today was to be the day of the Headmaster's execution.

She sat up slowly, rubbing the sleep from her eyes, and looked around at her friends who were all still sleeping. She didn't want to wake them just yet, but she knew they needed to start moving soon if they were going to prepare themselves mentally for the day's events.

Elara quietly stood up and stretched her limbs, trying to shake off the stiffness from sleeping on the hard ground. She looked up at the sky and saw that it was still early, but they needed to get going. She looked down at Rylan and gently shook his shoulder, waking him up.

Rylan sat up, his eyes still heavy with sleep. "What's going on?" he mumbled.

"It's time to get up," Elara whispered. "We need to talk about what's going to happen today. I know it's going to be difficult, but you can't run at the guards in some fool's charge."

Rylan rubbed his eyes and nodded. "Right, of course," he said, his voice still groggy.

"We're here to watch the execution in solidarity with Master Arin. We aren't here to save him and we aren't here to put ourselves in danger. We watch, and then we leave. Once we're done here then we'll head back to the Academy and see if we can try to warn the others about Captain Ren and the Air mages."

The rest of the group slowly woke up as Elara and Rylan spoke. They listened as Elara reiterated their plan for the day and the importance of staying focused and safe.

Kaelin nodded, her expression serious. "We need to remember that we're not just doing this for the Headmaster, but for all mages who are being oppressed by the King's regime. We need to be smart if we're going to make a real difference in the future. If we get caught, then there won't be a future for any of us."

The group felt the weight of their responsibility to their fellow mages heavy on their shoulders. They knew that this was just the beginning of their fight, and they couldn't afford to make any mistakes.

With a final deep breath, Landon got up, stretched and walked towards the end of the alleyway where the sunlight was bathing the main road in a warm glow.

Turning back to the rest of the group, he said: "Who's hungry then?"

"Are you joking?" Anya said. "I'm starving… but we can't risk trying to steal any food, can we? Or do you have some coins hidden somewhere I'd rather not think about?"

Landon grinned. "Actually, I do have some coins," he said, jingling a small pouch in his pocket. "I had a feeling we might need them."

The group laughed, relieved at the small bit of good news, but apprehensive in asking how he had acquired the money.

They walked out of the alleyway and onto the main road. The city was bustling with people, but there was an eerie quietness that hung in the air. It was as if everyone was holding their breath, waiting for what was to come.

As they walked, they saw that many people were dressed in black cloaks and seemed to be making their way to the centre of the city, which made moving around a lot easier than it had been before. As long as they kept their eyes down towards the ground, they shouldn't run into any trouble.

The city guards also seemed a little more absent and Elara assumed that they were busy preparing for the spectacle that was due to begin within the next few hours.

They made their way to a small bakery and entered the flimsy looking door, making a bell ring.

The smell of freshly baked bread and pastries wafted over them as they stepped into the cosy little bakery. The walls were lined with shelves full of bread and other baked goods, and the air was warm and inviting.

A friendly-looking woman behind the counter greeted them with a smile. "Good morning! What can I get for you today?"

Landon stepped forward and pulled out the small pouch of coins. "We'll take some bread and pastries, please. Enough for six people."

The woman nodded and began to gather up their order, wrapping it in paper and placing it into a basket. As she handed it over to them, she said, "Be careful out there today. It's a dangerous time to be wandering around the city."

"And what do you mean six?" Anya said loudly. "There's only five of us."

"Yeah, but I count as two," Landon said, flexing his arms. Elara couldn't help but laugh and Anya rolled her eyes.

"Do I know you?" the lady asked, interrupting the jovial nature of the group.

The group froze, suddenly alert. Elara exchanged a nervous glance with Rylan, wondering if the woman was one of the King's spies.

"I don't think so," Landon said cautiously and Elara watched as he pushed the mana from his eyes and looked up at the woman. "Why do you ask?"

The woman's smile faltered slightly. "You just seem familiar," she said, eyeing them suspiciously. "And with everything that's been happening lately, it's best to be cautious, wouldn't you agree?"

Elara felt her heart rate increase. Were they in danger? Was the woman going to report them to the guards? She looked at Rylan, silently urging him to come up with a plan.

Rylan stepped forward, a reassuring smile on his face and he, too made an effort to let the woman see his eyes as he pushed the mana from them. "We're just passing through," he said smoothly. "We're not looking for any trouble."

"Oh, I see," the baker said, and the group turned to walk away.

"But there is one thing," she said before they managed to leave the bakery and the mages all stopped in their tracks.

Elara turned to look at the baker and the flash of bright blue in her eyes was unmissable.

Elara felt a chill run down her spine. She knew what it meant - the woman was a mage, just like them.

Rylan turned back to face the baker, his expression guarded. "What is it?" he asked, trying to keep his tone neutral.

The baker's smile returned, and she motioned for them to lean in closer. "I know who you are," she whispered. "I'm part of the resistance. We've been watching you and we want you to come back and see us once this is all over. We need to help each other if things are just going to get worse."

The group exchanged surprised glances. They had been so focused on finding allies that they hadn't expected to stumble upon one so unexpectedly.

"What can you tell us?" Kaelin asked, her tone cautious but hopeful.

"Nothing right now but come and find me in a few days. You'll see. You have more friends than you may know in this city. Do not lose all hope after what happens passes."

The group nodded in understanding. They didn't want to put the baker or her group in any more danger by asking too many questions in a public place. But they were grateful for the unexpected ally and the potential for more help in their fight against the King's regime. Especially if they had more friends out there.

"Thank you," Elara said softly. "We'll find you once this is all over."

The baker nodded and watched as the group left the bakery, each lost in their own thoughts.

"What do you think?" Rylan asked Elara as the group retook to the streets.

Elara furrowed her brow in thought. "I think it's a risk, but it could also be worth it. If she's part of the resistance, she could have valuable information and resources that we need."

Kaelin nodded. "But we have to be careful. We don't know who else might be watching or listening. We need to stay low and avoid drawing too much attention to ourselves right now."

Rylan nodded, his expression serious. "Agreed. We'll wait a few days and then try to make contact with the resistance. In the meantime, we need to focus on paying our respects to the Headmaster. We owe him that much for sure."

The group continued to walk through the crowded streets, their minds filled with worry and uncertainty. They knew that their mission was dangerous, and they were all too aware of the consequences if they were caught. But they also knew that they couldn't just stand by and watch as their world crumbled around them.

"Are you ready to go?" Elara asked as she realised that the group were meandering towards the palace, and towards where the Headmaster was going to be brought out to be hung for his crimes. His crimes being that he was simply a mage in a place where being a mage was not allowed.

She saw Rylan's shoulders rise and fall once, then he nodded.

"Have you ever seen an execution before?" he asked. "I mean with the crowds and the cheering and jeering?"

Elara shook her head slowly. "I've never even seen anyone die before," she replied.

"My parents…" Rylan said slowly. "They were executed. Hung from the gallows just like Master Arin is going to be today."

Elara felt a weight of sympathy for Rylan. She knew what it was like to lose someone close, but to see them die in such a brutal and public way must have been unbearable. "I'm sorry," she said softly, placing a hand on his shoulder in a show of support. Suddenly her attention turned to the locket within her pocket. The locket that had belonged to Rylan's parents which she now held.

Rylan shrugged off her hand and turned away, his expression hardening. "It's in the past. We can't change what's already happened. What we can do is make sure that the same thing doesn't keep happening to innocent people. And after today, that is what I swear that we will work towards, with the help of the resistance."

Elara nodded in agreement. "You're right. We can't change the past, but we can change the future. And we will do everything in our power to make sure that the people of this kingdom can live in a world where they are not persecuted for who they are or what they can do."

The group continued on towards the palace, their resolve growing stronger with each step. As they reached the outskirts of the crowd, they could hear the sound of jeering and taunting, and Elara felt a lump form in her throat.

The crowds that surrounded the gates were already dense. A lot of the citizens were wearing black cloaks, but some wore what they would normally be wearing for whatever work it was they did. It seemed like most of the city were in attendance though.

Elara could see the gallows just within the palace gates. The gates themselves were open, but the crowds were being held back by a line of guards spanning the entrance. She let out a small sigh of relief when she saw that the Headmaster was still nowhere to be seen.

Kaelin nudged Elara and gestured towards a group of soldiers who were standing near the back of the crowd.

She turned to Rylan and Kaelin. "We need to be careful," she said in a low voice. "There are soldiers within the crowd."

Rylan agreed. "We'll keep an eye on them. But for now, let's just focus on finding a good spot to watch from, and well away from them."

They pushed their way through the crowds, their eyes scanning the area for a safe and discreet spot to observe the execution. After a few minutes, they spotted a small clearing within the mass of bodies, and they quickly made their way towards it.

Rylan took a deep breath and turned to Elara, his expression sombre. "I need to warn you," he said, his voice barely above a whisper. "Watching an execution is not something that can be easily forgotten. The emotions and feelings that you will experience, they'll stay with you for a long time."

Elara looked at Rylan, her expression concerned. "What do you mean?" she asked, her voice shaking slightly.

"I mean, seeing someone die like that, it's not natural. And watching it happen in such a public way, with people cheering and jeering... it's like the world is turning on its head," Rylan explained, his eyes flickering with a distant pain. "You feel helpless, and angry, and scared all at the same time. And then there's the guilt, the guilt of not being able to do anything to stop it."

Elara's heart sank at Rylan's words. She knew that watching the Headmaster die was going to be a difficult experience, but she hadn't fully understood the extent of the emotions that she would feel. "What can I do?" she asked, her voice barely above a whisper.

Rylan placed a hand on her shoulder, offering what little comfort he could. "Just remember why we're doing this," he said softly. "We're doing this to create a world where people like the Headmaster don't have to die for simply being who they are. We're doing this to make sure that the future generations don't have to go through the same pain and suffering that we have. And we're doing this to make sure that the sacrifices that people like the Headmaster have made are not in vain."

Elara nodded, feeling the weight of the responsibility on her shoulders. "I understand," she said, her voice filled with determination. "And I won't forget why we're doing this."

Rylan smiled at her, a small glimmer of hope in his eyes. "Good," he said. "Then let's do what we came here to do, and honour the Headmaster in the best way that we can. Besides, there's one more thing."

"What's that?" Elara asked with her eyes wide.

"You'll always have me," he said with a smile. "The times where I felt alone, like when I wanted to charge out to fight the soldiers in the forest, you'll never have to deal with that alone, because I'm never going to leave your side."

"Trust me, you'll get sick of the smell soon enough," Kaelin added, overhearing Rylan's words.

Elara couldn't help but laugh at Kaelin's comment, the tension of the moment momentarily broken. She felt grateful for the support of her friends, knowing that they were all in this together.

"You know, I quite like his smell," Elara said playfully.

Rylan chuckled at Elara's words. "Well, in that case, we'll have to make sure I stay nice and close, all the time," he teased as he wrapped an arm around Elara.

Kaelin rolled her eyes. "Can we focus, please? We're about to witness an execution, remember?"

"Nah, it's alright. It's what he would've wanted," Landon said with a smile of his own.

Anya didn't say a word, and even the playful tone of the group did nothing to change her stern and concerned expression.

The noise of the crowd abruptly began to change, and then fade away to nothing as a bell atop the palace began to ring.

Elara felt the change in the atmosphere more than she noticed the change in volume that the crowds were making. It was as though the entire world had been pressurised to such a degree that it almost made her ears pop. Finally, she saw what was happening to facilitate such a change.

The Headmaster was being walked from the palace main doors, along the short stone road to the gallows.

His wrists and ankles were bound and connected with short lengths of sturdy looking chains, and a guard on either side kept him moving in the right direction. Behind the Headmaster walked Captain Ren in his crisp white uniform, and behind him, King Roderick.

Elara had never seen the King up close, but he wasn't what she had been expecting. Short dark hair beneath a pointed crown of solid gold, regal red robes and the like were all to be expected, but he was smiling and waving to the crowd. He was *actually* smiling at what these people were gathered to witness.

Elara felt a wave of disgust wash over her as she watched the King's cheerful demeanour. It was sickening to think that someone could find joy in such a brutal and inhumane act. She felt a pang of anger and sadness for the Headmaster, who was being led to his death for simply being who he was.

Rylan's grip on her shoulder tightened, and she looked up at him to see his own expression clouded with anger.

It was as if the King had no regard for the value of human life or the suffering that his actions were causing, but Elara remained still and silent as they watched.

As the Headmaster was brought onto the platform, Elara noticed that he looked surprisingly calm, almost as if he had already made peace with his fate. It was a stark contrast to the screaming and jeering of the crowds, who seemed to be buoyed by the arrival of either the Headmaster or the King himself.

Elara turned to Rylan, her eyes filled with tears. "How can they be so heartless?" she whispered. "How can they enjoy watching someone die like this?"

Rylan's expression was pained, but resolute. "They've been brainwashed," he said softly. "They've been taught to fear and hate us, and to see us as nothing more than monsters. It's up to us to change that, to show them that we're just people like them, with hopes and dreams and families."

Elara nodded, understanding the truth in Rylan's words. But it still didn't make the situation any easier to bear. She watched as the Headmaster approached the gallows and stood before a guard who prepared to place the rope around his neck.

Chapter 21: Memento Mori

As the executioner placed the Headmaster's neck within the noose that hung from the gallows ready to accept him, the King held up a single hand to silence the crowds.

Finally, Elara could see the fear in the Headmaster's eyes.

"Loyal subjects of Avondale!" the King announced loudly and in a merry tone.

The crowd erupted in cheers, but Elara felt sick to her stomach. How could anyone be so callous as to celebrate the death of another human being? She couldn't understand it.

But then the King continued, his voice growing more serious. "Today, we witness the execution of a traitor, a criminal, a mage who defied our laws and threatened the safety of our kingdom. But let us not forget that his death serves a greater purpose. It serves as a warning to all those who would seek to disrupt the peace and stability of our great nation. Let it be known that we will not tolerate any form of rebellion or sedition. We will crush it, just as we have crushed this traitor today."

Elara felt a chill run down her spine at the King's words. It was clear that he would stop at nothing to maintain his power, even if it meant sacrificing innocent lives.

But it is not just this one man who is to blame for the troubles that we face."

He paused, allowing the words to sink in as the crowd murmured amongst themselves.

"My own father, your beloved last King, was murdered by a group of mages who promised to bring my mother back from the dead. They failed to keep their promise, and they are the reason that I, and every single one of you has lost a great King and Queen . The mages have proven time and time again that they cannot be trusted, that they are willing to use their powers for their own selfish purposes."

The King's voice grew more intense, his eyes scanning the crowd as he spoke and his happy demeanour fading away. "And yet, despite all of this, there are still those who would defend the mages, who would sympathise with their so-called 'plight.' But I ask you, my fellow citizens, how can we trust those who have betrayed us time and time again? How can we allow them to walk among us, when we know that they pose a threat to our very way of life?"

The crowd erupted into cheers and applause, and Elara felt a sick feeling in her stomach.

"But fear not, my loyal subjects," the King continued, his voice soothing now. "For we have taken steps to ensure that the mages will never threaten us again. We have outlawed their practice, and we will hunt down those who defy our laws. We will keep our kingdom safe, and we will prosper."

The crowd seemed as though the King's speech was the best thing they had ever heard, with whistles, cheers and shouts ringing out and as the King finished his speech, the crowd cheered even louder, and Elara felt a tear slide down her cheek. She knew that the fight against the King's regime was going to be even more difficult than she had anticipated.

Then the attention turned back to the Headmaster, and Elara's heart sank even further. She had known that this was going to be difficult to watch, but looking up at the gallows it was as though her entire world was falling apart. She spared a sideways glance at Rylan, who she could see was standing still with his jaw clenched and his eyes fixed upon the King in silent hatred. She took a hold of his hand and squeezed tightly, though he did not return the gesture.

The Headmaster stood facing the crowd with his eyes scanning the faces he saw there.

Then slowly he turned to the soldier that stood next to the gallows, ready to push the lever that would cause the ground beneath the Headmaster to fall away and end his life. Elara could barely watch.

A loud bell atop the palace chimed once, twice, three times and on the third chime, King Roderick nodded almost imperceptibly, and the Headmaster fell the short distance downwards to extend the rope, pulling it tight around his neck.

Something was happening in the crowd though. With the last ring of the bell and the final breath of Archmage Arin, sections of the crowd were beginning to separate and wide circles formed around people as they threw back their black cloaks. People who Elara could now see had bright colours contouring their eyes.

Green, red, and blue these people were clearly mages from differing schools but they were all working together to show solidarity to mages and also the Headmaster who had paid the ultimate price.

Elara's eyes widened in surprise as she watched the people in the crowd reveal their true identities as mages. She couldn't believe what she was seeing. Had they come to witness the execution in solidarity with the Headmaster, or was there something more at play?

She looked around at her friends, seeing the shock and confusion mirrored in their expressions. Rylan's grip on her hand tightened, and she knew that they were all thinking the same thing: what was going to happen next?

The King seemed to be taken aback by the sudden reveal, his eyes widening in surprise. For a moment, the only sound in the square was the gentle swaying of the Headmaster's body as it hung from the gallows. Then, with a loud cry, the mages began to surge forward.

Suddenly, there was a commotion in the crowd as a group of people began to push their way forward. Elara watched as they drew swords and daggers as they approached the unmoving guards. Then the first spells arrived.

A huge fireball burst in the air just before the line of guards, causing them to scatter in fear for their lives, while tendrils of water wrapped around their ankles and pulled them off balance and down to the ground. The earth beneath Elara's feet began to rumble as the stone road began to crack and buckle.

Elara watched as Rylan conjured his wooden sword, his face a mask of determination. Kaelin, Anya and Landon followed suit, and they stood together, ready to fight alongside their comrades.

The crowd though had begun to dissipate in a wild frenzy and before she could move to do anything, Elara found herself pushed to the ground and she struggled to get back up as bodies collided around her. She could hear Rylan shouting her name, but she couldn't see him through the mass of people anymore.

Just as she thought that all was lost, she felt a hand grab hers, pulling her up and out of the fray. It was Kaelin, her expression grim but determined. "We have to get out of here," she shouted over the noise.

"No," Elara said. "We have to fight."

Kaelin opened her mouth to object, but as she did so another huge fireball careened across the entranceway to the palace and impacted a group of guards that were moving slowly towards the rebel mages.

"Maybe… maybe we can win this," Kaelin muttered as she watched the mages and their armed comrades engage the guards. It looked as though the pairings would have been fairly even, even without the addition of the mages casting their spells from distance – with them, the tide of battle was firmly with the rebels.

Elara's heart raced as she watched the chaos unfold before her. She knew that this was their chance to fight back against the oppressive regime, and she wasn't about to let it slip away. She grit her teeth and ran forward, Kaelin by her side. As they joined the battle, Elara focused her energy, calling forth her mana. She watched as two soldiers ran towards a fire mage who was unaware of their presence, and she willed a protective dome to surround him before the soldiers arrived. She smiled as she watched the soldiers run into her dome, but could do nothing to penetrate it.

Then she turned to see Rylan engaged with a single soldier holding a long, shining sword and she moved to help.

Elara rushed towards Rylan and the soldier, picking a discarded sword up from the ground as she ran. As she approached, she could see the determination in Rylan's eyes as he parried and blocked the soldier's attacks and Elara saw an opening to insert herself into the battle.

She took the opportunity to strike, aiming for the soldier's unprotected side. The soldier was quick, however, and managed to dodge out of the way, narrowly avoiding Elara's blade.

Rylan took the distraction in stride though, and quickly dispatched their opponent.

"I always knew we'd make a great team," he said with a cheeky smile. "But now's not the time to stare at me lovingly Elara, we've got a fight to win!"

Another soldier turned to face Elara, his sword at the ready, and the two of them circled each other warily. Elara could feel her heart pounding in her chest as she prepared for the next strike, and when it came she parried it with practised ease. This was not like the beautiful dance that she and Rylan had partaken in the first time they had sparred, rather it was somehow clunky, hate-filled perhaps.

Then she saw the soldier's blade coming at her again in a second aggressive strike and she knew there was nothing she could do to block this blow. Her sword felt like it was miles away from being able to block the soldier's strike this time so she did the only thing that she could think of.

She dropped her sword to the ground with a loud clatter, and willed her skin to harden.

Elara put more effort into the spell than she had ever done before, begging her mana to cooperate and just as she felt her tiny seed grow and encompass her entire body, the blade struck her in the neck.

Falling to the ground, Elara's eyes were wide with total shock. Shock that she had managed to survive what should have been a fatal blow. She could do nothing but thank her mana for bending to her will and for saving her life.

As Elara lay on the ground, gasping for air and clutching at her neck, she could feel the slight trickle of her own blood seeping through her fingers. There was only so much damage that her weak spell could prevent, but nonetheless it had worked and she would live to fight another day.

That was, of course if the soldier who had sent her tumbling to the ground was not preparing another attack with his sword.

Elara knew that she had to act fast. She tried to stand up, but her legs felt weak and unsteady beneath her. She stumbled and almost fell but managed to catch herself just in time.

The soldier was advancing towards her, his sword held high, ready to strike and as his attack came, the tip of a sword appeared within his chest as another combatant took his life just in time.

This was only the second time that Elara had watched as the life was taken from another person, and so far, it hadn't got any easier.

As the soldier fell to the ground in a heap, Elara looked up at the person who'd saved her, and her mouth fell open as she recognised the cloaked form of Darien, and next to him, Mara.

"What…?" Elara managed to squeak out.

"Never thought we'd see you again," Darien said with a chuckle and Elara couldn't fathom how he was managing to be so jovial in this time of extreme danger, and with death all around them.

Mara stepped forward, her face stern. "We came to help," she said simply, and Elara felt a lump form in her throat. She had never been so grateful to see anyone in her life.

Rylan stepped forward, a relieved grin on his face. "Well, well, well," he said, clapping Darien on the back. "Anyone I should know about, Elara?"

"This… this is Darien, and Mara," Elara said in a small voice. "They are the ones who saved me from the Grimscale in the forest the first time, and showed me where the Academy was… but I had no idea…"

"Listen, we can talk later but right now we need to fight," Darien said with a shimmer of green lighting up his eyes. "If we can pass the soldiers, we can get to the King and all of this will be over."

With those words, Elara looked to the palace where the Headmaster still hung, and saw that although the King had retreated somewhat, he was still stood there, watching as people died right before him. He had a handful of guards surrounding him, but nonetheless all the time that he was out in the open, they had their chance.

"Looks like it's up to us again," Rylan said to Elara as he handed her a heavy sword. "But we'll have to hurry if we want to get there before Anya and Landon. He gestured over his shoulder and Elara now saw Landon casting his earth spike spell over and over, causing guards to fly off in all directions either struck by the spike itself, or pushed back as the ground erupted beneath them. She could see that Anya was casting the spell too, but on a somewhat smaller scale that seemed quite deadly to any soldiers in its path.

Explosions of fire boomed across the open battlefield, and each time flames cascaded into the air, it was punctuated by the screams of the soldiers who had been caught in its wake.

Small tidal waves of icy blue water washed soldiers away as they ran from the offensive spells that they apparently had no answer for, and it was clear to Elara that these soldiers were simply no match for the combined might of the mages from the three schools of magic.

Soldiers were falling to the ground all around them, but they were taking mages down too as the battle continued. Elara knew that when she tried to cast too many spells in quick succession that her mana waned and eventually failed, so if this carried on, then the mages would tire and eventually run out of energy.

"Let's make our way to the King," Elara announced as her attention returned to the group who all seemed to be watching her.

Rylan held his wooden sword high into the air and shouted.

"To the king!"

A cheer returned from the mages who all seemed to have heard Rylan and with what looked like a surge of activity, the battlefield practically swelled with a movement towards where the King stood, just behind the still open palace gates and his royal guard.

Elara and her allies charged forward, their swords and spells at the ready. The soldiers tried to stop them, but they were no match for the entire weight of the rebellion bearing down on them.

Standing and watching the enemy approaching, King Roderick seemed as though he didn't have a single care in the world. Elara didn't know if this was because he had accepted his fate, or if he had simply been shocked into petrification.

The rebellion shrugged off soldiers as they moved to try to intercept, but there were simply too many and no matter what they tried, the mass of mages made their way towards the palace gates.

As they arrived though, out trooped what must've been an entire legion of smartly dressed royal guard from behind either side of the gates and before the mages could stop in their advance, they crashed into the soldiers.

The royal guard defended themselves well, but did not look as though they were trying to kill the mages outright and Elara realised what was happening all too late as the soldiers from the previous field of battle began to close in on them from behind, trapping them between a wall of steel, and the royal guard at the palace gates.

Elara gritted her teeth as she watched a mage parry a strike from one of the royal guards. They were better trained than the soldiers they had faced before, and their armour made them much harder to take down. A second guard pushed the mage back though and as she stood in the crowd, she could feel that it was condensing into a tight grouping.

A few of the rebellion had begun to fall, but it was clear what this was. The soldiers were going to round up the rebellion so that in the end, there would be no survivors.

Elara's heart sank as she realised what was happening. They had been so close to victory, but now they were trapped and outnumbered.

But she refused to give up. She raised her sword and shouted to her allies, urging them to fight back.

The mages rallied around her, casting renewed spells and swinging their weapons with all their might. The royal guard fought back just as fiercely, but the rebels were determined to survive.

Elara saw a flash of green light next to her as Darien unleashed a powerful spell, sending several guards flying backwards. Mara was wielding a staff just as the Headmaster had, knocking soldiers back with each strike.

But for every guard they took down, it seemed like three more took their place. The rebellion was being slowly pushed back, inch by inch.

Elara felt a sense of desperation wash over her. They couldn't keep this up forever. They needed a way out.

Then as though it was an answer direct from the heavens, three mages grouped together one of each of the elemental affinities of earth. Gaya's Grace, the Eternal Flame and Winter's Vein each flowed out of their hands in their bright green, red and blue, cracking with energy as they met in a triangular form between the mages.

Elara's eyes widened as she watched the mages combine their powers. She had never even thought that something like this was even possible, but she knew that whatever these three were doing, it was going to be powerful.

The triangle of energy crackled and sparked, growing brighter and brighter until it was almost blinding.

The soldiers around them seemed to sense it too, as they hesitated for a moment, unsure of what was happening.

And then the three spells collided with a force that shook the ground beneath their feet. A burst of energy exploded outwards, knocking back anyone who was too close, but it seemed to weave around any of the rebellion who had mana within them.

Elara shielded her face from the blast, but she could still see the devastation it had caused. The soldiers were thrown back like rag dolls, and the ground was scorched and blackened where the spells had collided.

Thick roots exploded from the ground and immediately set ablaze as they snaked their way through the soldiers. Tendrils split off and grasped a hold of soldiers and guards and they screamed as the roots turned to fire, burning and blistering their skin as the spell felled everyone it came into contact with.

Elara felt a shiver run down her spine as she watched the spell in action. It was both beautiful and terrifying at the same time. She had never seen anything like it before.

As the roots and flames dissipated, the soldiers who were still standing looked around in confusion, dazed and disoriented from the blast. It was clear that the spell had been incredibly effective, and had completely turned the tide of the battle.

The spell hadn't finished though. The component from Winter's Vein, the water mana hadn't yet done anything at all and as Elara watched, the roots and fire receded and the triangle of light morphed into a bright blue. Then it folded outwards and separated into a ring of tiny shards of ice, hovering in the air.

Elara could feel the temperature drop sharply as the ring of ice shards formed in the air. She realised that the water mana component from Winter's Vein was finally taking effect. As she watched, the shards began to spin faster and faster, creating a whirlwind of freezing wind and then eventually, the shards of ice careened away from the spell in an explosion of blue mist in all directions. They were like arrows and as they travelled, they seemed once again to avoid the rebels in the battle, heading straight towards the soldiers facing them.

Elara watched in amazement as the ice shards shot out in all directions, seeking out their targets with deadly precision. She could hear the soldiers screaming in terror as they tried to dodge the sharp icy projectiles, but they were too late. The shards cut through their flesh and bone, leaving a trail of death and destruction in their wake.

Elara couldn't help but feel a sense of satisfaction as she watched the soldiers fall one by one. She knew that they were the enemy, and they had to be defeated in order for her people to be free. But at the same time, she couldn't help but feel a twinge of sadness for the lives lost on both sides. It made her feel a little sick that she had revelled in the soldiers' deaths.

As the last of the soldiers fell, Elara looked around at the aftermath of the battle. The ground was littered with the bodies of the dead and dying, and the air was thick with the smell of smoke and blood. Then all of a sudden, the rebels, only a handful of whom still remained let out a loud cheer and held their weapons aloft.

The King though, still remained watching behind his last handful of guards.

Then Elara remembered something that gave her goosebumps, and at that very moment, from behind the King stepped Captain Ren, and two additional air mages all dressed in the same white, royal blazers with golden buttons. Each of them had no hair atop their heads and they all wore blank expressions on their faces as they stepped forwards.

"NO!" Elara cried as the rebel mages began to move towards the three, but her cry was drowned out by the sound of boots on the pavement and the readying of weapons.

Chapter 22: Airbourne

Elara watched in awe as the two air mages moved towards them, their hands raised in an offensive stance. She could feel the wind picking up around her, and she knew that they were preparing to attack again. It was as though the very air around them all was growing thicker and thicker and she knew she needed to do something.

But before she could react, the air around her shifted, and she felt the force of an invisible barrier pushing against her. She tried to push through it with her hands up before her face, but it was like trying to move through solid stone and she could see that every single rebel in the crowd was being affected by the spell, all of them unable to move.

"What is this?" Anya said, but it sounded like her voice was being muffled by the air mages' spell.

"It's the air mages!" Rylan called back, raising his voice to a shout. "I don't know how they're so powerful, but this is crazy, isn't it? we need to do something!"

"How about you swing your stick at them?" Kaelin called out through gritted teeth, but Rylan simply ignored her.

The group were all next to each other once more, fighting for what was right as though they were one singular force. The air mages' spell wouldn't last forever, they all knew it, but they could already see the royal guard moving into position, ready to attack when the time came and the spell failed. And the guards didn't seem affected by the wind at all.

Then the flash of a fireball lit up the world around Elara, quickly followed by tendrils of green shoots and roots, splashes of water and long, sharp icicles. The spells that were being cast into the wind though, quickly dissipated to nothing as though the wind simply blew them away and loud groans came from the mages who'd cast them.

"How do we best this?" one of the mages shouted, but no one offered any reply.

But Elara could feel something. The air mages' spell was beginning to weaken, and she felt the pressure against her dissipating. It was clear that by dispelling the rebel mages' spells, the air mages' own spell was faltering. She took the opportunity to stand fully upright, her hands held high before her face and as she did, she watched as her friends joined her.

The smiles that the air mages had worn on their faces began to falter now, and it was clear to everyone that they wouldn't be able to hold on much longer.

Buoyed by their minimal success and the feeling of the barrier spell beginning to waver, the rebel mages threw everything they had at the air before them and although the spells didn't make it through, surely, steadily the spell faded and eventually died.

Then a new huge red fireball cascaded away from the battlefield towards the King, who stood next to Captain Ren, though as the rebels now began to run behind the offensive spell, Elara could see that the King did not seem fazed by the danger he faced. If anything, he looked pleased.

The fireball raced towards the King and Elara could see that it would impact him any moment, ending all of this oppression and this evil that had spread through the kingdom.

Then Captain Ren stepped forward and he did not have to raise a single hand before him to cause the spell to immediately disappear with a puff of smoke. It was then that Elara felt something that she had felt once before in the presence of the Captain – her mana shrunk down into nothing and simply disappeared. She tried to cling onto the last flicker of the little green seed she felt within her, begging it to remain, but it slipped away from her and left her empty inside. And by the lack of spells being thrown any more, everyone else was suffering from the same problem too. Both sides of the battlefield

Elara felt a moment of panic as she realised that they were all powerless against the power that Captain Ren commanded. He was simply too strong as a mage to be fought. She looked around at her friends, their expressions mirroring her own fear and uncertainty. It seemed like all their efforts had been for nothing.

But then, something unexpected happened. The King stepped forward, his expression calm and measured. "Captain Ren," he said, "enough. The rebellion is over."

Elara watched in disbelief as the Captain turned to look at his King, his stern expression softening slightly. Everything turned silent and the rebels were immediately surrounded by the royal guard, their weapons lowered menacingly. The battle was over.

"These rebels will be made an example of," King Roderick said with a sneer. "That no matter how strong a group may think they are, they will never stand toe to toe with my royal guard."

Captain Ren's face betrayed a flash of distaste at not being recognised as the reason for their victory in battle, though if he had anything to say to the King, he kept it to himself.

Elara felt a wave of despair wash over her at the King's words. It seemed like their fight had been in vain, and that they would pay dearly for their actions. But even in the face of defeat, she refused to give up. She looked around at her friends, seeing the same determination in their eyes.

"We may have lost this battle," she said loudly, her voice shaking slightly. "but the war isn't over yet. We'll keep fighting until we're free from this tyranny. You're a monster, King Roderick! "

Her words seemed to resonate with the other rebels, and they stood a little taller, their expressions more resolute and a few muttered words of agreement rang out.

King Roderick's sneer instantly turned into a scowl. "Take them away,' he ordered, but the rebels all took a shuffling step back from their oppressors.

"You'll never take us alive!" the shout came from the midst of the crowd, and it was greeted by cheers of agreement.

The King held up his hands in a silencing gesture. "If you wish to die, then so be it," he said and he gave a tiny, almost imperceptible nod to Captain Ren, who unsheathed a long, silver sword and stepped forward.

Elara felt her heart race as the Captain moved with his sword in hand. She knew that they were completely outmatched and outnumbered, but she wasn't ready to give up just yet. She looked at her friends, seeing the fear and determination in their eyes.

"We fight to the end," Rylan said quietly to her, his voice steady.

Elara nodded. They might not win this fight, but they could make a stand and show that they were not afraid to fight for what was right. At least that could give other mages hope for a better future.

Captain Ren led the charge, his sword held high with a mischievous grin on his face. As he approached, Elara raised her hands and tried to call forth her mana, though no matter how much she begged, it still did not respond.

Whatever Captain Ren was doing, it apparently didn't require his full concentration.

The resumption of the battle was as fierce as it had ever been, with swords clashing against swords and armour in a deafening crescendo. Elara could feel the energy of her comrades draining quickly, but she refused to give up. She could see that her friends were also pushing themselves to their limits and that soon they would be overthrown.

"We'll take you all on!" Rylan shouted as he parried a guard's attack. His voice was surprisingly steady and Elara could see that his hands had turned white around a very metal looking sword.

Captain Ren laughed, a deep, rumbling sound that echoed through the square. "You rebels are all the same. Foolish and naïve," he said, and without warning, he lunged forward, directly towards Rylan.

Rylan met his attack head-on, their swords clashing in a shower of sparks. Elara stood back, unsure of what to do next. But then she saw Anya, Landon, and Kaelin standing together, their hands joined in a circle. They were muttering under their breath, and Elara realised that they were doing whatever they could to try to coax their mana back to their bodies.

As the three mages worked together, Elara could feel the energy in the air changing. The wind picked up, and the ground beneath her feet trembled. Captain Ren, distracted by the sudden shift in the air, turned to face the trio and in that moment, Elara saw her chance.

He had been so preoccupied with fighting against Rylan, that when Elara swung her sword, she knew that there was nothing the air mage could do to block her strike and as the sword came closer and closer to her target, she felt belief swell up within her.

Then as the blade was no more than an inch from its target, a pulse of air burst out from the Captain and everyone around him was thrown back at least a few feet and to the ground.

"You think that you can defeat me?" he shouted.

Elara slowly rose to her feet, shaking off the impact of the Captain's spell. Her ears were ringing, but she could see that her friends were also getting back up, and they all looked determined to continue the fight.

"We don't have to defeat you," Elara said, her voice ringing out clear and strong despite the chaos around her. "We just had to distract you."

"Hell yeah!" Landon shouted, fist pumping the air and Anya covered her eyes and shook her head.

Captain Ren sensed the change, but before he could sap the mana from the area once again, Elara saw a multitude of spells being cast all at once from all of the rebel mages.

Reds, greens and blues lit up the battlefield as soldiers and rebels fell in the first swathes of renewed battle. Something hit Captain Ren, throwing him to the ground and Elara could see that although he was down, he wasn't out of the fight just yet, his chest still rising and falling steadily. It was a lucky hit nonetheless to remove the skilled Captain from the fight, at least momentarily.

But then the rest of the guards were still surrounding the mages and even as the numbers fell on both sides, they closed in. The soldiers though had the upper hand, and within a moment unless something big happened, the fight was going to be over.

A soldier dispatched a mage next to Landon as he and Elara locked eyes. Her friend was too close to the menacing armoured man now bearing down on him but there was nothing she could do.

Landon then cupped his hands and unleashed his most favoured spell.

"NO!" Elara shouted as she watched the soldier run Landon through with his sword, now coated in her friend's deep red blood.

But Landon's spell had already taken and the ground beneath Elara's feet began to tremble.

As if in slow motion she then saw Anya casting a spell as she too was cut down with a spray of her own red blood leaving her body. Then Kaelin also found herself on the wrong end of a soldier's sword and she fell to the ground as she weaved her mana into a spell of her own.

The ground beneath Elara's feet opened up, and a sharp spike of pure earth mana forced her high into the air. Guards were instantly impaled by the spell that her dying friend had cast and as she rose into the air atop the spike, she could see that below, the battle had already been lost. More soldiers were arriving and the last of the mages had begun to fall.

The spike would have impaled Elara, too, but for the last spell that Anya and Kaelin had each cast: Protective wooden domes surrounded both her and Rylan as they were shot high into the air and away from the city. Their wooden domes acting like bubbles that protected them as they flew through the air and eastwards towards the Forbidden Forest. Anya, Landon and Kaelin had each given their lives so that Elara and Rylan would be safe from the result of the battle.

Tears streamed down Elara's face as she realised that her friends had given their lives so that she and Rylan could escape.

She looked across to the second wooden dome that flew beside her own. Rylan gave her a small smile, and she felt a glimmer of hope in her heart. They might have lost their friends, but the war wasn't over yet and they would not let their friends die in vain. They would keep fighting, keep pushing forward until they achieved their goal.

Rylan then mouthed the word 'harden' to Elara as he pointed down to the ground and within a second she had recalled her mana and cast the spell.

Together, their wooden domes hit the ground within the forest hard, and immediately shattered into thousands of pieces.

Elara lay on the ground unmoving, before she coughed and spluttered. The pain she felt was almost unbearable but then she turned her head to see Rylan lay on the ground bloodied and broken. She knew that she was in a bad way too, but she found herself unable to move or even speak.

Within her hand, she held tightly the locket that Rylan's parents had given to him before they had died and she smiled internally. In her short life, she had made friends, had a purpose, and sometime in the future, she knew all of this oppression would come to an end.

Then a rustling sound came from above her head and she hoped that whatever it was that had come to find her would be merciful, ending her life quickly and painlessly. But as she wished, something even better happened: a familiar beaked, feathery-scaled face appeared above her, looking down where she lay.

The last thing that Elara would see before her vision faded to black, were the curious faces of two large, and one juvenile Grimscales.

Epilogue

"I want every last one of those rebels to be punished," King Roderick said, his voice low and menacing. "I will not tolerate any further dissent in my kingdom."

Captain Ren nodded, his face grim. "We will make sure that they are dealt with accordingly, Your Majesty."

Elara's parents, Serena and Marcus exchanged a worried glance. They had seen Elara within the city, and they feared for her safety. They had not approached their daughter, though, for fear of being overseen by any of the guards of the soldiers. It was lucky that they had been allowed to work their debts off by the palace as it was.

The pair stood to the side of a long corridor and only happened to overhear the conversation between the King and Captain as they returned to the palace following the great battle by the rebel mages.

Serena's heart was heavy as she thought of the fate of the rebels and her daughter. She knew that Elara had been a part of the rebellion, and she feared for her daughter's life. She looked over at Marcus, her husband, who was equally concerned.

"What are we going to do?" she whispered to him, her voice shaking.

Marcus looked around nervously, making sure that no one was within earshot. "At least we know there are more rebels in the city now, perhaps all is not lost?"

"You mean if they were not killed in the battle?"

The pair hushed again as they heard that the King was again speaking to Captain Ren.

"I want to know where these rebels came from," he was saying in a harsh tone. "I want to know if there are more. I want you to personally look into the eyes of every single man, woman and child within this city and I want every single mage that you find brought to the stronghold."

Serena and Marcus exchanged another worried look as they realised the severity of the situation. They knew that Elara was not the only mage in the city, and they feared for the safety of all of them. They needed to find a way to warn their daughter and the other rebels of the impending danger.

"I promise you, my King," Captain Ren replied. "The only mages that will survive this culling, will be the air mages under your control."

King Roderick was silent for a long moment before he replied, his tone now calmer and dripping with subtext.

"You know, I despise all mages. I despise the fact that you all seem to twist things to your own benefit, but what I hate most of all is the liars that you all seem to be. Trust me when I tell you this my Captain: when your usefulness to me and this city comes to an end, you will not escape the same fate that the rest of these rats will face under my rule."

"I think it may be time for us to leave this city," Serena said to her husband.

"But before we leave, we need to do everything we can to warn any of the mages or rebels still around. We can't just let them get rounded up and executed, can we?" Marcus asked.

Serena nodded, her mind racing with possibilities. "But how do we warn them without drawing suspicion? We can't just go around shouting it from the rooftops."

Marcus thought for a moment before an idea struck him. "What if we spread rumours? We can start whispering to people that the King's soldiers are rounding up mages and rebels, and warn them to leave the city as soon as they can."

Serena's eyes widened with realisation. "Yes, and we can tell them to pass the message along quietly to others they know. That way, we can warn as many people as possible without drawing too much attention. And perhaps the rumours will spread beyond the city walls and further afield."

Marcus added: "We need to be careful, though. If we are caught, we'll no doubt be killed."

Serena nodded. "We'll have to be discreet. We can start by talking to our friends in the taverns and ask them to pass the message along to others."

When the evening came and darkness would shroud their movements, the couple set to work, spreading rumours, whispers and warning people of the impending danger. They knew that time was running out, and they prayed that their efforts would be enough to protect at least some of the mages and rebels in the city. They also knew that they couldn't stay in the city for much longer, so they made plans to leave the very next day, as long as their rumours were sure to be spread.

The next morning as the sun rose, they were preparing to leave their makeshift quarters within the palace. It was small and uncomfortable, but at least it was free after the city had taken their farm away in payment of some of their debts.

There was a quiet knock on their door and the pair exchanged a worried glance before Marcus went to answer it. Opening the door, he saw that it was one of their friends from the taverns, looking both anxious and scared.

"What are you doing here, Robert?" Marcus asked.

"I came to tell you that the rumour has been spreading like wildfire through the city," he said quietly. "And I wanted to let you know that there are a lot of people ready to follow your footsteps out of the gate and into the beyond. Is the plan to leave immediately?"

Serena was taken aback by the announcement; they were not leaders of some great exodus from the city.

"We're leaving now," Marcus confirmed. "But in truth, we have no idea where we're going."

"Well, there was one other thing," Robert said balling his hands nervously. "In the battle, I saw your daughter Elara." She didn't die," he added quickly. "But I saw her thrown clear and over the city wall in some wooden dome. I don't know if she could've survived, but it seemed a little convenient to me."

Serena gasped, a glimmer of hope in her eyes. "Elara... thrown over the wall? In a wooden dome? Are you sure?"

Robert nodded. "I saw it with my own eyes. I don't know what it means, but I thought you should know."

Serena and Marcus exchanged a worried look. They knew now that they had a purpose: to find their daughter, and they were willing to do whatever it took to bring her back to safety.

"Thank you, Robert," Marcus said. "We'll keep an eye out for any signs of her. And we'll see you by the gates shortly. Tell everyone you can that we are leaving the city, and we won't be coming back."

Robert nodded, understanding the urgency of the situation. "I will spread the word," he said before hurrying away.

Serena and Marcus quickly gathered their belongings and set out for the city gates. They didn't really know where to start, but they were determined to leave no stone unturned.

When they arrived at the gates, the pair of guards let them pass right through. It was strange, there was nobody awaiting their arrival so they simply kept going. They had warned the people in the city as best they could, but if their daughter was injured, or in trouble then they could waste no more time.

After a few minutes of walking, they came face to face with hundreds of people standing in wait for their arrival.

Serena and Marcus were taken aback by the sheer size of the crowd that had gathered. They had not expected so many people to join them on their journey out of the city. The crowd was made up of mages, rebels, and ordinary citizens who were all looking for a way out of the city before the King's soldiers started their culling.

"Are you leading us out of the city?" one of the mages asked Serena and Marcus with a hopeful expression on her face.

"We're just trying to find our daughter," Serena replied. "But we'll do what we can to help everyone get out safely."

The crowd murmured in agreement, and the group started moving eastwards and towards the Forbidden Forest; it was the only place that Elara could've fled to after being thrown from within the city.

Serena and Marcus were grateful for the support of the crowd, but they were also worried about the dangers that lay ahead. The Forbidden Forest was known to be a treacherous place, filled with all sorts of beasts and dangerous magic and even the soldiers seldom travelled within. They knew that they had to be careful, and they made sure to keep the group together as they made their way towards the forest.

But as a group, they knew their chances of both surviving, and finding Elara were greatly increased.

It would not be long before they stumbled across the broken remnants of the wooden cages that had carried Elara and Rylan out into the forest, though they would not be occupied by either.

End of Book 1

A Thankyou

Again, your investment of your own time and money is always well appreciated and again, I ask that you **rate** and **review** everything that you read – and not just this book, so that lesser-known authors can grow their audience and gain the credibility that they deserve for their hard work.

Also, check out my website, it's usually kept up to date with current works, reviews and a few extra little bits. You'll find it at:

www.davidlingard.com

Thank you